AF614420

SOUNDS OF WONDER

John Holland

AuthorHouse™ UK Ltd.
500 Avebury Boulevard
Central Milton Keynes, MK9 2BE
www.authorhouse.co.uk
Phone: 08001974150

This book is a work of fiction. People, places, events, and situations are the product of the author's imagination. Any resemblance to actual persons, living or dead, or historical events, is purely coincidental.

First published by AuthorHouse 02/25/2011

ISBN: 978-1-4520-3400-3

This book is printed on acid-free paper.

Dedication

Sounds of Wonder is dedicated to
all those who love and respect
the countryside and wild places
and who cherish the flora and fauna
that inhabit the natural environment

ACKNOWLEDGEMENTS

I would like to record my thanks to the following for their advice and assistance:
Shona Campbell of the Gaelic Society of Inverness,
Sinclair Coghill, Deer Officer from the Deer Commission for Scotland,
the staff at AuthorHouse for their excellent support and particular thanks go to my sister Janet, for resolving many of my computer-related problems.

CHAPTER ONE

The first year would be critical. As Chris and his wife, Amy, huddled together near the glow of the wood-burning stove, it seemed a good time to reflect upon the wisdom of their move north.

Of course, there would be problems and tensions with such a venture. But they had moved from tension-ridden, work-driven, mind-numbing monotony, stuck on a characterless estate in the heart of Midland's soulless suburbia. Chris was fortunate to have had twenty-five years' continuous employment in the Defence Ministry, until they closed the depot where he worked. He had felt trapped in a claustrophobically routine job, which he tolerated simply because he feared the consequences of jacking it in. His redundancy had changed things; when his workplace closed, he had no decision to make — change had imposed itself.

*

Twenty months had passed since his pointless paper processing had ground to a halt. The redundancy money eventually percolated through and in a few years his occupational pension would be payable at sixty. In the meantime, a long-forgotten Premium Bond brought £25,000 of luck. Surely things were meant to change. They would have a lot of thinking to do. Amy's skills exceeded Chris's, but would her yoga teaching and some catering experience secure enough regular income for the two of them? Chris was in his fifties, and getting another fulltime job would be difficult; he wasn't the most likely of candidates to be "head-hunted."

The enchantment of their neatly manicured leylandii had faded long ago, together with neighbours who swept up autumn's fallen carpet of resplendent gold, russets, and ochre with a vacuum cleaner. To keep their sanity they had to move, but where? They couldn't afford a move to the deep south. He had heard of one or two that had done so, never to be seen again, swallowed up in anonymity. It had to be north, over the border. At least their mortgage was paid up.

Perhaps they could buy a place somewhere in the glens and run a bed and breakfast business from it. Amy's culinary flare would be essential and Chris fancied he could handle the accounts, take the bookings, nothing too strenuous. Having holidayed in the Highlands over the years, it was clear that spending two weeks there in June was a different ballgame to living there, year in year out. They had also gathered that it is nigh on essential for incomers to be practical and resourceful in order to eke out a living. Amy had the idea of listing the pros and cons of their intended scheme. Fairly high on the cons side was a reference to Chris's somewhat narrow — some would say untapped — skills base. Still, in the absence of any brighter idea, they were committed.

Then followed a cramped and cluttered existence in a draughty caravan down a Scottish track for six months while the money from the house sale came through. It seemed an interminable time for them; a daily round of mopping up condensation, trying to dry clothes, and juggling three pans on two cooker rings. They vowed never again to take a well insulated house for granted; heat loss was terrific. Already, life in the Midlands seemed light years away. Their time in the caravan was filled with two main preoccupations: not to succumb to bronchial problems (which they managed to avoid), and looking for a well insulated property that was big enough to take guests.

The location had to be right; it was no good offering good bed and breakfast if it takes an expedition to find you. Driving through the village of Inverdruie, their attention was drawn to a sale board flapping in the wind. Behind it and nestled between a copse of Scots pine and a bubbling burn was a granite-built house with dormer windows at the front and a well stocked lean-to woodshed to its side, giving the place a welcoming feel.

"Inverkeld" was engraved in the granite door lintel. Their first impressions of the house were good and they exchanged nods.

"Worth a look inside, Chris, don't you think?"

"Reckon so. It says 'Enquiries to the Post Office' on the sale board."

Two hundred yards into a freshening damp westerly brought them to the post office.

"Aye, an' whit canna be doin' far ya?" enquired a lady with grey, curly hair as she peered over her spectacles. A couple of minutes and a phone call later and they had the estate agent's property details and the keys to inspect Inverkeld.

"You'll be sure te return the keys before I close, now?"

"Certainly, many thanks, bye for now."

*

The house was in good condition, and having just been vacated was virtually ready to move in to. Chris tried to hold back the disappointment at not being able to unleash his DIY talents, but Amy had seen this act many times before and just gave a wry smile. They had already sold their suburban wonder house and the accepted offer was processed to completion as they neared the end of their tether in the caravan.

By early September they had the keys to move in to Inverkeld and their first act of faith was to trust that the wood-burning stove would be reliable through the Scottish winter. It was. The kitchen was a spacious square shape with a big, black, *olde-worlde* cooking range, which would be essential for Amy to do several breakfasts together. Those shortening autumn days were spent unpacking crates and boxes of belongings that had been in storage. It was chaotic but it was definitely better than crawling in and out of dank sleeping bags in the caravan days. They knew it would take all of those winter days to graduate from chaos to organised chaos, and it did.

By early springtime they had achieved some semblance of being settled.

"When do you think we'll be ready for our first guests, Amy?"

Four bedrooms could be used — one double, one twin-bedded, and the two single dormer rooms at the front, and all these were ready for guests. Chris and Amy slept in the room at the back, adjacent to the kitchen.

"I think we should try for early summer, Chris, but you will need to organise the publicity."

The first guests booked in to stay at Inverkeld in May of that year. Chris's contacts in the Midlands came in handy, as did Amy's computer skills. Even Mrs McGuillvary at the post office played her part; word of mouth counted for a lot in those parts and news travelled like a raging bushfire.

*

Chris reached over and fed another log into the stove. It was October and they had survived their first season doing bed and breakfast. At weekends Amy provided dinner for those guests who wished it, although the Claymore in the village also served good food and ale. It was clear from the early days, however, that they would have to generate more income.

One idea was to offer dinner with bed and breakfast through the weekdays as well as weekends. All they needed was extra help. Their second idea was to deploy Amy's cooking talents further by opening for lunches, based on good, honest home cooking using locally bought produce. Again, this was beyond their labour pool of two, which meant that their plans would have to be put on hold.

It was getting late and they were too tired to come up with any solutions. Then, part way through their turning-in routine, the phone call ...

"Hi Mum, it's Ben. Sorry to float this one past you, but I'll be finishing my uni course at the end of this term — any chance I can stay with you for a while?"

Amy was flabbergasted. It went deadly quiet. She was usually very good at thinking on her feet, but this time she sat down. "Well, I suppose so, son. It all seems a bit sudden, is anything wrong?" Her voice wavered with anxiety.

"No, it's okay — just that things don't seem to be working out with my course. Think I need a change. Oh, and will it be okay if Karen comes up with me?"

"Y-yes, my love, just give us a ring next week and let us know when to expect you."

"Cheers, Mum, must go now. Speak to you both shortly, bye."

*

Three weeks later Amy and Chris welcomed back their prodigal son, Ben, and his partner, Karen. Just as the elders were beginning to get things straight, their household had doubled. Of course, things weren't that bad; they were pleased to see Ben again and made him welcome. It transpired that Ben's health had started to suffer as a result of studying and exam pressures. He had been reading zoology and music. His parents were gutted to hear that his studies had come to such an abrupt halt. Their feelings of disappointment — seasoned with some anger — were tempered by those of just wanting their only son to be happy with himself. But he must first regain his psychological strength.

If it was a change he was looking for, Chris and Amy agreed he would surely find it there. They certainly had. Perhaps the crystalline northern night skies, with their purity undiminished by intrusive city lights, would help. It would take him ages to become accustomed to the noisy silence, a permanent background of tumbling energy from the nearby burn, punctuated by gusts and groans of the Highland winds.

Karen was a year older than Ben and had graduated in zoology the year before. Amy and Chris were both happy with Karen from their first meeting; she had a stabilising influence on Ben and she was bright, level-headed, and was of a friendly disposition.

Those weeks prior to Christmas were inevitably a bit tense, because so many things were uncertain; how was the bed and breakfast business going to turn out? How *long* were the youngsters going to stay and *what* were they going to do?

CHAPTER TWO

Amy and Chris weren't looking forward to this sudden change to their routine; they expected the young arrivals to do a lot of hanging around in the house and to get under their heels somewhat. To a point, this turned out to be the case. However, following the initial newness of the situation, family life began to evolve into some kind of pattern.

They agreed that Ben and Karen would occupy the double bedroom upstairs. Of course, by doing so, it had drastic consequences on the B & B guest rooms available. They had to do something; this arrangement could not be permanent, and they all knew it. It would have to do for a while, but a better solution would have to be found before the start of next spring's tourist season.

Financially, it was clear that Chris and Amy could not afford the cost of an extra two voracious appetites unless the young ones earned some money. These were ideal conditions for propagating a divisive tension within the family. Conversely, the situation could bring out the best in them; it might indeed make their relationships stronger.

Certain house rules had to be established early on. Even before their arrival, Amy and Chris anticipated that the youngsters would be habitually late in getting out of bed. Ben would certainly have fallen into this pattern, but he was, thankfully, under Karen's strong influence. Indeed, this "Karen factor" would prove to be beneficial, as time unfolded.

Seven-thirty was not the best time for Amy and Chris to hear what Ben was so keen to announce at the breakfast table.

"Karen and I have been thinking, well, you know the Wildlife Park higher up the glen?"

"Yes, Drumrowan Wildlife Park."

"That's it. Well, they are recruiting staff to take on for the start of this coming season in April. Even better, they have offered Karen and me jobs with them!"

Chris chipped away at the broken shell 'round the top of his boiled egg for a second or two. They could envisage Karen getting off her backside and securing a job so quickly, but the *two* of them?

"That's great news, Ben." Amy was first to reply. "Tell us, what will you both be doing?"

"Training will start in March and we'll both be doing hands-on stuff, which is what we want. According to the job description, we will be involved with the routine, daily welfare of the larger mammals and also be part of the Rangers Service, meeting the visitors."

Chris was anxious to ask how many hours they would be employed for. Until Ben's breakfast table exposition, he had hoped that Ben and Karen would help with the bed and breakfast business, and Amy was of the same view. If they were to join them as part of their team, they could build up the business. Alas, such hopes were evaporating fast.

"Karen," Chris said, "have you any idea of the hours you, er ... what days, I mean, will it be part-time or —"

"Oh get on with it," Amy cut in.

Chris continued, "Well, do you know what hours you will be working, Karen?"

"Basically five days a week including every third weekend. Initially we will be taken on for the summer season, possibly leading to year-round work after a review in six months."

The ringing of the phone broke everyone's train of thought and Chris shuffled across to take the call, an accommodation booking enquiry. After tidying the breakfast things away, the youngsters left the room, leaving Amy and Chris to distil this new information.

*

It was seven-forty as the early morning bus pulled up at the drive. Karen and Ben were ready. The driver was taciturn; he crunched his way into first gear and the vehicle lurched forward. A couple of small windows had been left open overnight and hoar frost had to be cleared from the glass with gloved hands in order to see anything. It was like being in an icebox. Hard tyres shattered the ice crystals over ruts and potholes in the deteriorating road. An uncomfortable eight-mile journey took them three hundred feet higher up the glen to Drumrowan Wildlife Park. The ancient bus rattled over the buckled bars of the cattle-grid at its entrance.

Glad to get out, the two youngsters surveyed their new working environment. Dense, blue-grey clouds settled low along the slopes. There was a pervasive stillness, with cloudlets of frosted breath rising from the groups of red deer and Highland cattle. It was their first day of work and things looked different from when they attended for interview, weeks ago. On their interview day, they were only shown 'round the Visitor Centre and offices; there had not been time for an outside tour. They were to report to the Head Keeper, Callum McNeish.

Across the courtyard, a black door-latch clanked up and a young, fair-haired man emerged and strode purposefully toward the newcomers.

"Hello," he called, "are you Ben and Karen who are starting with us today?" He greeted them with a smile.

"Yes, hello."

"My name's Jamie, and I've been expecting you. You'll be wantin te see Mr McNeish — I'm his assistant. Come with me, I'll take ye over."

They made their way 'round the end of a fine row of granite cottages, knocked, and entered a side door.

"McNeish is the name, Callum McNeish. You'll be the new starters, I take it." He rose from his chair, thrust out a hand, and clamped poor Karen's fingers painfully in his strong grip.

"Y-yes, we are. Pleased to meet you. I'm Karen and this is my partner, Ben," freeing her fingers as she spoke.

"Partners, mm ... so you'll nae be wed yet? Still, we needn't go into all that. Jamie, if you'd care te carry on an' we'll meet up after lunch."

"Fine, Callum, see you later."

Jamie gave Karen and Ben a smile and went on his way.

"I've just made a brew, would ye like a mug?"

"Please."

Drawing on his pipe, the tall, sixty-three-year old Keeper put three mugs on his draining board and swivelled round to examine his new charges.

"Sit yerself doon."

His white hair and heavy eyebrows contrasted with rusty, weathered skin, his dark eyes inset above a high cheekbone. An old scar showed on his left jowl, just to the side of his white moustache.

The office phone rang during their tea-break, and McNeish relayed the message.

"That was Lord Cameron. He and his wife are the owners of Drumrowan Estate. He was just askin' if I had your job descriptions and a couple of Health and Safety forms for you both to sign. We might as well do them while we're finishing our tea."

"Oh yes, we were interviewed by Lord Cameron and also met Lady Cameron. They seem very pleasant," said Ben.

"Indeed they are good people, all reet. If you're finished yer tea we can have a look at the indoor animal enclosures, and then I was intendin' te drive ye 'round the Estate grounds."

"Thank you."

Their eyes had only just adjusted to the soft hues of his cosy office, with winter morning light slanting through two small windows and suffusing with the pervading, calming aroma of pipe tobacco smoke. The mounted head of a ten-pointer stag adorned one wall. McNeish had a large hardwood writing desk with a substantial carved chair, an envelope-opener with a deer-bone handle, a paperweight of smooth Torridonian sandstone, and a selection of pine cones. Ben wished there was more time to look round his office; it was a shame to leave.

Outside McNeish's headquarters everything was a lot brighter.

"We have the 'domestics' — the rabbits, goats, saddleback pigs, an' what have ye, in this big area here. It's excellent fer families, an' the kids enjoy feedin' an' strokin' them. One o' me lads, Davie, looks after this side o' things."

"It's obviously a very big operation here, Mr McNeish" remarked Ben.

"Certainly is. The whole thing is what ye see here, an' then there's the Visitor Centre with its café, the larger mammals in the parkland, an otter compound, woodland trails, holiday lodges, and a vast upland acreage. Some of the red deer are farmed and other herds range free on the hill."

"Heck, it's really amazing!" enthused Karen. "How many years have you worked here, Mr McNeish?"

"It's Callum to you. It'll be more than twenty, but I'll retire in a couple of years and I'm trainin' up young Jamie to take over the reigns. Lord and Lady Cameron fully approve — he's a likeable lad."

They boarded McNeish's Land Rover and drove off through the parkland. In it, there were enclosed areas for deer, Highland cattle, lynx, wild boar, llamas, huskies ... and wolves. The deer were free to roam in the park but had a secluded sanctuary area of their own. McNeish pointed to a Scandinavian-styled wooden lodge in the parkland.

"That's where Mikel lives, a Swedish chap in his fifties, who came over to settle in the Highlands many years ago. He pays a peppercorn rent to the Estate in return for 'adopting' the huskies and drivin' them as a sledging team three or four times a week. He's a very likeable fella."

The grand tour was over twenty miles long and took them through broadleaf woodland, conifer forest, moorland, and craggy, open mountains. On their return, McNeish took his charges to the café and made sure they were given staff discount. They agreed to meet back in his office after they had eaten. Their cheeks and noses were numb with cold and it was good to be enjoying hearty Scotch broth and steaming drinking chocolate.

After lunch, McNeish explained about the feeding requirements of the different animal groups, plus helping and looking after the visitors, natural history, environmental awareness, safety, security, and the Estate vehicles.

"We open the main gates to the public at nine-thirty in the mornins. I live in the cottage set well back from the main drive. Feel free te use any o' the three Land Rovers, the keys are kept in my office — we call it the 'lair.' Time is gettin' on, so we'll drive through the park and do a final sweep, making sure all visitors are back at the car park area."

The Keeper's dark brown eyes glinted piercingly into Ben's and Karen's. "It's of vital importance that we check and secure all the animal enclosures with this electronic device 'ere. It's all high tech and linked to a control panel in the lair. So, you'll 'ave 'ad enough by now. If we see ye in the morrow at eight-fifteen — that's when I 'ave me daily briefin' — I know that after another hard frost, the first job will be to grit the main drives and paths. I'll bid you good day, then."

Fifteen minutes later, Ben and Karen were on the return bus back down the glen.

"He's a bit fierce, isn't he?" Karen said.

"Intimidating — I'm not sure about him either," replied Ben. "Still, tomorrow is another day and it might take a while to get to know the old fox."

*

The next day, McNeish's team of four was assembled dutifully and on time in the lair. With Ben and Karen were Jamie and Davie, the keeper in charge of the smaller animals. To Ben and Karen, it seemed there was a hell of a lot of ground to cover and things to do for only five of them. Callum explained that the keepers worked closely with the Rangers and there was a fair bit of flexibility. By chance, the door swung open, and in stepped a strongly built woman in her early fifties, bringing in with her a wake of swirling snowflakes. This was Morag Strachan, the head Ranger. She shook her long, fiery red hair as Callum introduced her.

Karen was to help Morag load the trailer with animal feed and replenish all the feeding points in the large animal enclosures. This was quite an elaborate procedure, in that a different food mix had to be prepared for each of the animal groups. Meanwhile, Ben was trusted to work with the gritter, with Jamie showing him the ropes. There had been an overnight dusting of snow down to valley level, and an easterly wind had lifted the cloud-base to above three thousand feet, and extensive snow-fields that were concealed yesterday now showed themselves.

During those first weeks, Ben and Karen made a good start at Drumrowan. They were both working on the same days, which was good for them. Much of the work was, of course, routine but there was always something different happening. At the first opportunity McNeish introduced them to Donald Bell, the local vet from Inverdruie, whilst he was on a routine visit to Drumrowan. He had a contract with the Wildlife Park for regular visits in addition to emergency calls. He was a sixty year old, of average build, who wore thick-lensed glasses and had a long, white, untrimmed beard. Most folks referred to him as the "vetranny."

Lord and Lady Cameron's family home was an impressive building, turreted, with a castellated wall. It was set in its own gardens and commanded an elevated position several hundred yards from the public areas. The Camerons were active gentry people who made an effort to see their staff on a regular basis and had a hands-on approach to the running of the Estate. It was Cameron philosophy that if you were genuine, trustworthy, keen, and prepared to work, you would do well. Conversely, if you just played at the job, you were asked to work your period of one month's notice. To a large degree, McNeish had been brought up with the same doctrine. Therefore, to Karen and Ben there was a consistent approach coming from above; they knew what was expected of them.

CHAPTER THREE

Back at Inverkeld, the range of mealtime conversation had expanded well beyond ordering sufficient eggs for next week's breakfasts. It was stimulating for Amy and Chris to hear how their son and his partner were getting on. They had noticed Ben was steadily regaining his lost self-confidence, and from what he told them, his boss was giving him responsibility and the trust that goes with it.

Easter was only three weeks away and accommodation bookings were building up. Amy and Chris had been worrying about this; the inescapable fact was that there weren't enough rooms!

Amy whispered, "Chris, we really *must* tell them how serious it is."

Chris took the initiative. "Ben, Karen, we've got a crisis on our hands with the bed and breakfast bookings. We simply don't have a bloody clue where we'll put our guests over Easter."

"It's not quite *that* bad, Chris," interjected Amy, "but we will have to do something quickly."

Karen took this opportunity by saying, "Ben and I thought this would be a problem and we've been discussing it. At Drumrowan there is this small cottage which has been unoccupied for months. It's well away from the other buildings and a bit spooky."

"It has a wood-burning stove, I had a peep inside," Ben added.

"Well, there you are, problem solved," Chris replied.

"Hang on, Dad, we've not even mentioned it to Mr McNeish yet and we've only been working there for a month."

"He's right, Chris, it's an awkward situation for them," Amy said, trying to help.

"Oh don't *you* start on me too. Anyway, I've enough worries with my egg order and where the hell I am going to put Mr and Mrs Bell on the 24th." Hopelessly outnumbered, he went into one of his huffs.

Karen eased the atmosphere by agreeing to ask Mr McNeish if they could rent the cottage. She and Ben found themselves in a crisis of their own; they would have to speak with McNeish tomorrow, but their timing had to be just right — and time was running out.

*

Huddled together on the bus, one thing was on their minds.

"We'll have to ask him right after his briefin', Ben."

"Yes, it's our only chance, love. Just hope his phone doesn't ring at the wrong time."

Oddly enough, McNeish asked them to stay back after his briefin'.

"You've now been with us for a month. This is when we review how new staff are gettin' on. I have to give a progress report to Lord and Lady Cameron. Well, you're doin' fine; you're good grafters an' the other staff an' the public seem te like ye. You'll 'ave seen the Camerons down 'ere quite regularly — they don't miss much. They are very pleased with you both. So ... that's the review over — any questions?"

Karen took a quick breath; she knew this was their chance. "Well, Callum, we've noticed that cottage at the entrance to the parkland, it doesn't look to have been lived in for a while."

"Aye, that wee place, it's nae fit fer man nor beast."

"Ben and I are having to find a place of our own pretty quickly," she continued. "Would there be any chance of us renting it?"

McNeish took his time to rekindle the rutilant embers in his beloved pipe.

"Bloody hell, ye must be desperate — an' what's the almighty rush?"

Karen summarised their domestic situation at home.

Once he realised that there was no new baby on the way, McNeish fully sympathised with the youngsters' predicament. "When would ye be needin' te move, in the summer?" he enquired.

"Before Easter really, Callum."

"Hells bloody bells! THIS Easter? If ye get crackin' on with yer jobs, I've a hell of a lot te sort out. I'll be seeing the Camerons with yer progress report, so I'll see what they say."

"Thanks very much, Mr McNeish," they chanted in unison and left the room in total bewilderment.

As they expected, McNeish summoned them before him the following morning.

"I've 'ad a word with the Camerons an' they think yer idea aboot the cottage is a good one. They will instruct the contractors workin' on two of the holiday lodges te make it habitable and they'll insist it's done pretty damn smartish; no one tends te argue with Lord and Lady Cameron. I'll 'ave a wander across te check how much needs doin' — it shouldn't be too much."

It was agreed the couple would pay only a peppercorn rent and by the end of the following week the place was still pretty dusty and in need of new curtains but otherwise ready to be occupied.

*

Ben was out in a Land Rover on one of the forest tracks when he swerved and just missed a jeep which had cut straight across him. Out jumped Morag Strachan, the head Ranger.

"Hi, Callum's asked me te have a word with you, Ben."

"Oh hello, Morag," he replied, still dazed after his emergency stop.

"Just call me Mo. Callum's arranged for me te bring the trailer doon te yer house tomorrow, to take whatever ye need te the cottage, so you'll nae need te take the early bus. I'll see ye tomorrow then. Cheers!"

"That's great, Mo," he replied, but before they agreed to a time, she shot off again in a cloud of dust.

The following morning there was frenzied activity, with parents and offspring all pitching in, loading up sleeping bags, duvets, books, mountain bikes, essential clutter, electrical stuff, cds, dvds — even a camping stove: the belongings of two untidy youths. Amy and Chris were pleased that Ben and Karen had found a place of their own and were excited for them. But it did mean that, without them, they could get back to muddling along together in their old ways — and could now make that double bedroom available for their guests!

On their next free day, the twosome moved into their new abode. A pair of roe deer antlers was mounted above the black, wooden door, which led straight into the main room. Cobwebs spanned the corners of the low ceiling. Faded mesh curtains hung by the small, wooden-framed windows. In front of the wood-burning stove stood an expensive looking bottle of red wine, with a card signed by Lord and Lady Cameron — a really kind thought. In the middle of the stone floor was a tarnished, rectangular wooden table with two upright chairs. An old rocking chair stood by a small, pine dresser, with a meagre collection of crockery laid on it. One door led through to the wee kitchen with its electric cooker, and then to the bathroom and toilet. The other door connected with the one double bedroom, which had a black fireplace and open chimney in its end wall. They remembered Callum saying that this chimney was in good condition and that they could use the open fire. The bed was three-quarter size: on the mattress, there was a pile of folded blankets and a couple of sheets and pillows. The young couple were thankful of having brought their own cosy duvet.

After sorting out some of their things, they went outside. The lean-to woodshed by the side wall had been fully stacked with logs.

"There were no logs here the other week," Ben remarked. "I'll bet good old McNeish has seen to it."

*

Ben and Karen began to stir from their fitful sleep. The bedroom curtains had not been drawn together and the first rays of winter's morning sun beamed through across their bed. They could relax because they had another work-free day. Their bodies were pressed firmly together; only their noses were cold. Facing together, they exchanged smiles and watched clouded globules of their condensed breath drift upward and merge together, something Ben thought was very intimate and erotic.

Eventually, Karen sat up and shook the thin coating of damp rime from the duvet. They had both been too tired last night to light the stove or the fire, so getting dressed was painfully cold. After breakfast, Ben laid some paper and kindling, brought in some logs, and lit the stove. Callum had suggested they keep the stove lit for a couple of days to warm the place through.

Their midmorning coffee break was interrupted by the sound of skidding tyre rubber, followed by a terrific clatter. Karen peered out; it was Mo, who had come up with Davie. Ben opened the door to greet them.

"Hello, Mo, Davie."

"Good mornin', are ye settlin' in alreet? We've brought up a settee on the trailer for ye, as I noticed ye might be a bit short of chairs an' seats."

"We *are* actually, Mo," replied Karen, "that would be fantastic, thanks very much indeed."

The four of them made easy work of moving the two-seater settee inside. It had seen better days, but it would do fine. Mo and Davie didn't have time to stop, but they agreed to meet up for a coffee sometime.

*

Karen and Ben had enjoyed their second free day at the cottage. Tomorrow they would be back at work and the following days would lead straight into the busy Easter period. It was dark when they finished their evening meal, but they decided to have a short stroll before turning in. Donning warm clothes and wellies, they picked up the two hurricane lamps from the windowsill, lit them, and set off. Already they were beginning to appreciate the big difference between just spending their working hours at Drumrowan and living on that magnificent estate all the time. They felt part of the place; they had learned to live *with* the natural environment and to care for everything that lived alongside them.

Some lights were on at the Visitor Centre. A curling string of white lights lined the path linking the holiday lodges. A full moon was up; moonbeams shone through between high, wispy cirrus. There was a sharpness in the cold air. The quivering hoot of a tawny owl carried from the woods above the burn. Now and again, they would hear the huskies as they settled down for the night.

Occasionally, the wolves would break the silence with their wondrous sounds, which stopped the couple in their tracks — wild, searching calls, so evocative as to strike right to the heart of one's soul. It was as if their howling was reminiscent of humankind's long-lost free spirit.

This was a magical place they had come to; everything was completely new; it afforded them so many exciting things. Kicking off wellies and snuffing out the lamps, they stripped off, dived under the duvet, and snuggled in close; life was good.

*

Easter was late that year, the third week in April and all parts of the Wildlife Park were working to capacity. The eight discreetly located holiday lodges were all occupied. There were many visitors enjoying the good weather, and the Ranger Service, headed by Mo, was particularly busy. In addition to their other duties, the Rangers provided a daily Guided Walk, lasting about three hours.

A fair amount of snow had receded during the past fortnight; the valley floor was quite wet and the burns were brimming with melt-water. Clusters of primroses were in flower on the lower, sun-facing slopes and wood anemones — "wind-flowers" — carpeted the woodland floor.

Ben and Karen enjoyed their first Easter at Drumrowan. Having passed their review period successfully, they were given extra training in the Rangers' duties, and this was carefully planned so that they were able to assist the Rangers over Easter. They found some of the work physically tiring, but it was interesting and they felt they were part of a good team.

CHAPTER FOUR

In early May, Mo kindly offered to take Ben up onto the moor, to watch black grouse displaying. It was a chance not to be missed. Mo warned him it would mean a very early start — she was to call for him at four-thirty! Ben was apprehensive. From what he had seen of her so far, Mo was energetic in everything she did and this dynamism explained why she was often seen flying about the place. At first he found it rather stressful working with her because of this. He expected her to shoot off in her jeep at terrifying speed, race along the forest tracks like a demented rally driver, jog across the moor, and make so much noise the birds would be long gone.

He couldn't believe it. There was a gentle rap on his front door at just turned four-thirty. He didn't even notice her jeep pulling up. After whispered welcomes, Mo moved off smoothly, staying in second or third gear. They exchanged greetings with Mikel, who was out early, driving his husky team.

"God morgan (goo morron)," called the flaxen-hared Swede as he sped off amidst a cloud of vaporised husky breath.

Mo brought the jeep to a halt by a stile, and they proceeded on foot along a faint track across the moor. She pointed to a curlew flying overhead, emitting its beautiful, bubbling, aqueous call. In a few hundred yards, she gestured for them to lie down and crawl forward. A damp mist hung round the heather.

It was like being with another person. Mo was in her element as a wildlife Ranger; whenever she was out in the countryside, she moved with stealth and grace and spoke softly; Ben was learning so much from her. He was later to read entries from the Visitors' Book, which bore testimony to her communication and natural history skills:

"Excellently led Guided Walk."
"Miss Strachan showed us so much, thank you."
"The nature walk was the highlight of our visit."
"Our children were thrilled when they were given pine cones
the red squirrels had eaten from."

They were looking at ten male black grouse — blackcocks — at their display area.

"This is their lek," whispered Mo.

The females stayed on the periphery, watchful for the most impressive males. Transfixed, they watched as the blackcocks strutted and stamped about, making weird sounds as they ran mock charges at each other. They would then turn to display their splendid, white fanned-out tails. It was awesome.

After a while, the action began to tail off.

"Put yer binoculars doon," whispered Mo.

In a flash, she rolled poor Ben over onto his back. It was so quick. She slid a hand down his trousers, held him, and made no effort to retract. She let her breasts settle in Ben's cupped hands and let her weight fall on him. Pulling herself down to him, they kissed. He realised she was just as strong as he was. After a minute, she rolled back off him.

"Sorry about that — didn't mean te upset ye. Are ye alreet, Ben?" she enquired, as she flicked her fiery hair.

"Urr ... think so ... yes, I'm fine, thanks, Mo."

Nothing much was said on the way back, but Mo was very relaxed about what had happened and this helped him. He couldn't understand it. They respected each other before and that would not change. Perhaps the "fling in the heather" had released an underlying tension between them. In time, they became great friends; when they were out working together they were a strong team, and they both knew it.

For weeks, Ben was fearful of when Mo might again overpower him with her fiery passion. Fortunately, she never did — that is, nothing more than a friendly slap on the backside. As for Karen, she never got to know. Ben simply didn't have the heart or the nerve to be honest with her and perhaps it was just as well.

Some time later, Ben was chatting with young Jamie in the café during their lunch break. "What's your opinion of Mo? How do you find her, Jamie?"

"Everyone gets on with Mo. She has a heart of gold, very caring, and someone ye can really rely on in a crisis. Oh, some folks used te think she was a bit of a nympho, but I don't believe it."

"Oh," Ben replied thoughtfully.

CHAPTER FIVE

Amy had organised the upgrading of rooms at Inverkeld in the first year of their bed and breakfast business. She and her husband concentrated on providing good quality accommodation and food. However, it soon became apparent that most of their guests were looking for something more; they asked questions about the area and its wildlife:

"Are there any Scottish crossbills nearby?"
"Where is the best place to go to see red squirrels?"
"Have you ever seen a pine marten?"
"What are the small birds with long tails feeding in your garden?"

It was in their interest to know what was going on; guests expected it and looked to them for local information. Pretty quickly, Amy acquired a selection of natural history books, local booklets, and trail leaflets, which she arranged in a corner of the cosy visitors' lounge, and she also bought a pair of binoculars. Before long, Amy and Chris were not just providing a high standard bed and breakfast but were giving their guests a "Highland Experience." Paradoxically, by providing this Highland Experience, they were gaining from this very thing and felt closer to their natural surroundings.

Something else happened which was to further influence the couple; visits to Drumrowan Wildlife Park galvanised their feelings for nature and enriched their lives. Occasionally, they would take advantage of cancelled B & B bookings by spending a day with Karen and Ben at Drumrowan, when they both had a day off work. Naturally, Karen and

Ben welcomed them to their cottage, and the two couples explored the Estate on each visit.

One such day was in June. The foursome were relaxing over mugs of coffee in the cottage after an evening meal which the youngsters had made. Chris and Amy enjoyed seeing them happy and still in that huggy-kissy stage of being in love. To finish the evening they brought out some photos of the cottage before it was occupied. Those faded curtains had been replaced, but the old, stained table was still the centrepiece of the lounge. From the experience of previous visits, Amy and Chris had learned to take their chance with the atrophied — nay, knackered — padding of the settee, rather than risk one of them being pitched out of that notorious, unstable rocking chair. The warm glow from the wood-burning stove cast distorted shadows across the well-worn, russet rug. Flickering, scented light emanated from a couple of Karen's candles. Karen and Ben had made changes, but they hadn't tarted the place up; it still oozed with character, and they were evidently delighted to be living there.

As Amy and Chris were shaping up to leave, Ben said, "Come through to the bedroom, there's something you might like to hear."

Amy caught her husband's eye with a "what the devil is he on about?" look. In turn, they stood on a stool in the far corner of the bedroom and pressed an ear to the wall — Ben first, then Karen, followed by Amy and Chris. Without Karen's commentary, Chris and Amy would have struggled, but yes, they could just make out faint scrabbling sounds.

"We have a colony of bats staying with us!" Karen proudly announced.

"I wouldn't have guessed, just by the sound," replied Amy. "It's great, but how did you notice they were in your roof?"

Ben was dying to get a word in. "On one of our evening strolls we spotted them flying from a small crevice in the roof. What we're hearing is the bats moving about, getting ready to emerge for a night's feeding."

"If we go outside we can watch them — they are pipistrelles, Britain's smallest bat," added Karen.

They went out into the gloaming and didn't have to wait. From a small crevice, singly or in twos and threes the bats launched themselves into the night sky on their feeding sorties. Chris started to count them but soon gave up. He was spellbound for a minute. "They're so small, such a rapid, erratic flight — incredible."

It had been a memorable day.

*

Later in the year the family spent another day together at Drumrowan and were returning from a stroll through the Estate parkland. The huskies, in their large enclosure, were no doubt thriving in the frosty conditions, their dense, creamy coats melding with the surrounding snowscape. Amy and Chris particularly enjoyed walking over to the fenced but extensive, rocky, wooded, undulating area to see the wolves. It was especially moving to be there with them in the twilight of a winter's day. The couple would hold hands and say nothing as the wolves came closer, moonbeams reflecting off their dark, glistening eyes. Occasionally, an adult would send out a protracted, low, sonorous howl, gradually ascending into a sustained, high-pitched whine, which would carry through the cold, crystalline air ... through to one's very soul.

Back at the cottage, they warmed themselves through with mugs of coffee before Amy and Chris would have to return down the glen to Inverdruie. Ben and Karen had kept their stove burning; flickering orange pervaded round the room, lighting furniture and faces. From the tassels of the russet rug appeared Humphrey — the name Karen gave to one of their spiders. A year ago, Chris would have tried to kill it. Now he was pleased to see him; he and Humphrey were getting on together just fine.

Of all the animals at Drumrowan, Karen's favourites were the Highland cattle. She loved being close to them, as when she gave them winter hay fodder. Karen looked into their dark, half-hidden eyes as they nonchalantly took the fodder. Mouth and nostrils exuded cloudlets of condensing breath into the clear, cold air. On sunny, spring days, steam rose from their shaggy, double-coats of dun or orang-utan red. There was something timeless about these "Highlanders," and they had a majesty which set them apart from other cattle breeds.

After such a day, Karen was chatting to Mo in the Visitor Centre café. "I took a few photos of the Highland cattle when I was giving them their winter feed," Karen said. "They are fantastic, docile beasts."

"Aye, they are," replied Mo, "I've a fondness for them too. Mind you, have ye ever wondered how Callum got that curved scar on his left cheek? It was one spring-time an' he somehow got too close to a cow with her calf. She slowly swung round an' caught him with her vast, spreading horns."

"Ben and I *had* wondered about Callum's scar," Karen said.

Mo added, "Still, Callum had no ill feelings for the animal, it was his own daft fault, she was simply being a good, protective mother."

*

The self-catering lodges at Drumrowan were situated along the fringe of a large swathe of Scots pine. Red squirrels lived in the woods and they would regularly come to the bird-tables. Visitors were thrilled when they saw a hunched ball of sunlit fur working at a pine cone with its sharp, dexterous forepaws.

That year, a couple of pine martens had started to make evening visits to the lodges. This caused quite a stir as they had not been seen in the area before. Lights from the lodges shone into the gloaming. The stage was set. Guests staying at the lodges had nothing to do but stay still and quiet, savour red wine and wait. If their luck was in, a dark-chocolate coated, lithe, sinuous creature would emerge, approach cautiously and with one athletic spring, land on the feeding platform and scan 'round for signs of danger. Its prize was usually various treats covered with peanut butter and lots of fruity jam. The long, dark brown tail was eye-catching, but its distinctive feature, surely used in display to other martens, was its conspicuous gorget, the pale, pastel shade of ripening rosehips.

Staff at Drumrowan were looking forward to a second year with the pine martens. Only twice had two martens been seen together, but there was speculation as to whether there could be a small breeding population.

By mid March of that year, preparations were going well in the run up to Easter. The cleaning ladies had worked overtime in order to make the holiday lodges ready for the new season. Guests who had booked the first available week were enjoying sunny weather, and things were going well for them. Well, things went without incident until the Friday morning ...

Callum was out on his rounds. His radio crackled into life: "Callum, it's Jamie. Would ye mind popping back to Reception, we've got a lady who's in a bit of a state."

"Okay, Jamie, I'm on me way."

McNeish did his best to calm the lady down; she was seated and sipping sweet tea, surrounded by a crowd of well-wishers who towered over her. The poor woman was so distraught, it was as if she had witnessed a murder.

When she was calm enough to speak coherently, she explained that she was driving slowly between the holiday lodges and her car struck an animal.

"I think it's dead; it didn't move afterwards. It had a long tail, so I suppose it was a fox." With that, teardrops continued to drip from her nose into her teacup. McNeish and Jamie exchanged a look of horror — they doubted it was a fox. Immediately, they almost pushed people aside, jumped in Callum's jeep, and sped up to the tragic scene. There it was. They looked down and shared a quiet moment together, two grown men almost reduced to tears. Callum knelt down and cradled the pine marten in his strong, brown hands.

"Hey, wait a minute, it's still warm. I wonder if there's just a chance ... Jamie, we'll take it down te the Visitor Centre an' phone the vet."

Jamie held the creature while McNeish drove as though his life depended on it.

"Donald, thank the Lord yer in, it's Callum. Can ye get yerself up here reet away, I've got a mart that's been hit by a car an' I'm not sure if we can save it."

In the time it took Donald to bundle his stuff together and trundle his old van up the stony approach road, McNeish, Jamie, and Mo had prepared space on the stainless steel surfaces in a room Davie used for the smaller, "domestic" animals. Ben had put the injured creature under his coat, trying to retain its warmth.

"Should I keep the marten in my jacket, so it stays warm, Callum?" he asked.

"Aye, that's a good idea. Yer doin' fine, Ben. By the way, we just call 'em marts 'round here."

Donald arrived shortly, and he quickly set to work. "It's struck its head on the vehicle; you'll see dried blood coming from the ear. It's nae so good." He checked for breathing and any sign of life and let out a heavy sigh. "She's dead but she's obviously pregnant. I'll see what I can do; I'm going te open her up. Mo, can ye pass over my leather holdall, please?"

In a few minutes he was asking for warm water and dry towels. He cleaned up two blind, helpless creatures, enveloped them in the towelling, and instinctively passed them to Mo. Everyone was struck mute, even Donald with his nearly thirty years' veterinary experience.

"We're breaking new ground here, but the first priorities are warmth and food," Donald said. Mo, who had her arms full, delegated Jamie to get one of the plastic rabbit carriers and line it with straw, while the "vettnary" proceeded to close the dead animal up.

"I know young marts are completely dependent upon their mother for the first six weeks," Callum explained, "so feedin' them is goin' te be a real headache. Obviously, the young will need round the clock care at first an' I'll happily put together a rota, but as te what we'll feed them on ..."

"Can I suggest we try warm goats' milk te start with," Mo said. "It's more easily digested in the stomach than cows' milk."

"That seems to be as good as anything, Mo," Donald replied.

Callum rearranged tasks for the rest of the day. Naturally, it fell upon Mo to take the first nightshift, and she was last seen carefully carrying one occupied rabbit box, towelling, a blanket, cartons of goats' milk, and an assortment of feeding bottles to her place.

*

There was no shortage of volunteers to help with looking after the two young marts. Lady Cameron insisted that Callum included her in the team of helpers; she thought nothing of having a few of her nights interrupted by regular feed times, and her staff felt the same.

Donald the vettnary was in daily contact by phone. The martlets were weighed regularly and managed to make it through that first crucial week. Before long, Mo, after checking with Donald, gradually introduced them to the more fortified nutrition of condensed milk. The young martlets readily took to accepting their bottle-fed nourishment and showed a healthy weight gain. During the day, they were kept in a quiet area behind Reception, beyond the reach of excited children and always under the care of a nominated member of staff.

Within the next two months, the plan was to relocate the martlets in the woods near to where their mother had been found. To prepare for this, Callum had assigned Jamie and Ben to make a wire enclosure with a built-in cat-flap arrangement which could be secured as necessary. The lads built this at the chosen release site. Within the enclosure, they made a roofed, wooden shelter which they clad with rocks and earth and generously lined it with straw in an attempt to simulate a dark, well insulated breeding den. Things were looking good; before long, the martlets could be moved to their newly constructed accommodation in the woods.

The young marts were outgrowing their indoor surroundings, and the time was right to relocate them. Callum and Mo drove them up to their new quarters on a warm, sunny morning. In the weeks to come, they would be left a daily supply of eggs, nuts, fruit, muesli, and wholemeal biscuits. It would be fascinating to see how the youngsters would attain the necessary skills to hunt and kill in the absence of their mother. Time would determine whether they would survive the first winter. The plan was to provide food for and monitor the martlets daily, keeping the cat-flap in the enclosure secure. When they were behaving independently enough, the cat-flap would be left open, enabling the youngsters to range into the forest. They should then be ready to forage from nature's autumnal harvest.

Without fuss, Mo and Callum placed the open transit box in the enclosure, retreated to a nearby cushion of bilberry, and waited. Callum ran a finger through his white beard.

"As you'll be aware, Mo, we're nae goin' te radio-tag the martlets."

"Aye."

Callum continued, "That'll mean our best way of monitoring them in the wild is by visual recognition. It's likely that the shape and size of one mart's creamy gorget — its 'bib' — is different to another's. So, if we can recognise this in our two youngsters, we might be able te identify them in the wild."

"That's where some of the photographs we've taken will help," Mo added.

"Exactly, me bonny lass."

"Hey," Mo interjected, "they've both emerged from the transit box and into the enclosure. I'll take some final pictures while I can." When she was satisfied with her camera work, the two of them reluctantly boarded the jeep and made their way down the dusty track. It was in the lap of the gods as to what the morrow would bring for the orphaned bundles of mischief.

During the ensuing weeks, the martlets were provided with daily supplies of food. Eventually, a scat was found by Callum in the area surrounding the enclosure. Following this proof that the marts were venturing into the forest, the food they were provided with was reduced to a subsistence level. On daily visits to their enclosure, the marts were seen only on some days. Less and less was seen of them until there were no more sightings. They would have to take their chance and run the gauntlet of survival, with shortening days heralding the approach of winter.

CHAPTER SIX

Drumrowan Estate farmed red deer, and these animals were kept in several fenced areas on the flattest land adjacent to the river Bhruie. There was increasing demand for the supply of venison to hotels and restaurants throughout the region. Indeed, Chris and Amy had started to order Drumrowan venison to include in their evening meal menus at Inverkeld.

However, in autumn the focus of attention was with the wild red deer on the hill. An important source of income was from clients who paid for the opportunity to stalk and shoot prize stags. The general pattern of things was that shooting days were booked, usually well in advance, by paying clients. They were looked after by McNeish (who was once a gillie) and the Rangers, who tried to ensure their guests had a good sporting day out in pursuit of their quarry. At Drumrowan, the aim was to achieve a balance between maintaining a good annual sporting income and sustaining a robust, healthy deer population and the neighbouring estates had similar objectives.

During this time, the subject of red deer was to dominate many of McNeish's briefing sessions. They were busy weeks, with commitments to meet with shooting days and all the arrangements that they entailed. Anyhow, all the clients, many of whom made this their annual pilgrimage, went away happy.

Straight after the end of the last day's successful sporting shoot, there was a distinct easing in the atmosphere around the place; there was still much to do, but the first part of the deer season had gone well. The pressure was off and there was an end-of-term mood in the lair, and Callum's briefings were more casual. He now seemed to draw on his pipe more from pleasure than necessity. The pervading pipe smoke had a hypnotic, soothing effect and his faithful team were all beginning to drift. Through the blue-grey mist, Callum proceeded to outline plans for what was one of the highlights of the year at Drumrowan, the red deer rut. Rutting would reach its peak in the next fortnight and several events, at which the public were invited to observe the rut, were organised around this.

Young, fair-haired Jamie, Callum's assistant, had found an excellent place from which to watch the competing stags. Small, excited groups of up to six guests were driven high up the glen. Jamie's favourite observation point was along a track that cut across the heathery hillside above the upper waters of the Bhruie. They left the mini-bus at a turning area. "From here it's only a short uphill stroll to the *bealach* — that's Gaelic for a pass or saddle," Jamie explained.

At the bealach the group was able to take up position behind a rock outcrop, which was shoulder high and an effective screen from the deer but afforded good views of them. Most clients had their own binoculars, but for those without, they could be hired from the Visitor Centre. Jamie proudly brandished his telescope and was keen for his clients to get a more detailed view of the action.

Everyone attending the red deer rutting events returned back to base exhilarated, not just by privileged views of those magnificent animals, but also by sounds of their deep, bellowing roars resounding in the glen. Occasionally, they could even hear the dull clash as opposing antlers engaged! Days like those were the easiest part of the Rangers' job; they didn't really need to do a great deal to please people. Nature did that.

*

In addition to the October deer rutting events, Lord and Lady Cameron had come up with another initiative. Their idea was to have sound recordings made of red deer stags at the time of the rut to be played through speakers in the Visitor Centre during the rutting season, thereby adding a striking audible dimension to the deer photographs already on display.

McNeish was asked up to the Camerons' residence about once a month — it was mainly a social invitation with a bit of work thrown in. He had been with them for coffee and toasted crumpets topped with cream and raspberry conserve — oh, and to hear of their new idea.

Back in his cosy black-beamed cottage, McNeish pondered, over a dram of his favourite malt, on how to get the recordings done. Jamie, Ben, and Karen would be ideal for the task, and he invited them over to his cottage the next evening.

It was Ben and Karen's first visit to Callum's cottage. He had just lit his stove and was relaxing in his rocking chair. A *forte* passage from the glorious, lilting, final theme of Beethoven's Pastoral Symphony boomed out from his portable radio. As his guests knocked and entered, Callum turned down the volume but didn't turn it off — after all, it was Beethoven. The threesome knew that there was something big to be asked of them, the moment McNeish offered them a dram of his treasured malt. He explained what was required.

"I realise it's nae goin' te be an easy task. Angus, my friend from the Forestry Commission has offered to loan us outdoor recording equipment, and he'll kindly get it over te me in the mornin'. Time isn't on our side as the rut will start te tail off during this coming week. The weather forecast is none too good, but do you think you'll be able te go for it, the day after the morrow?"

Jamie had seen the forecast and it was to be bloody awful. He glanced at his mates and nodded at Callum with his bright, blue-eyed smile; it was on. However, they knew there was far more to come when McNeish came round with his bottle and plied them with refills.

"It'll take ye te the remotest part of the Estate, that's why we'll need three of ye. Jamie, I know ye love yer mountains and have been up lots of Munros in all weathers; I'll rely on you te look after everyone. You'll have two mobile phones between ye, but the signal's dodgy oot there. The waters will be in spate, so I reckon the worst bit might be crossing the rope-and-plank bridge, you'll know it, Jamie."

"Yes, Callum," he replied, "the old ropes have been replaced by two steel handrails, but it's still scary, especially in a wind."

Callum continued, "As a precaution, I'll give ye this short rope, Jamie, as you have experience in tying-on and belaying. Ben, if you take yer walkie-talkie, I'll be in hourly contact with ye. Think of it as a wee adventure, and you'll be fine."

Callum had placed great trust in them, but he knew they would be sensible, and for their part his charges would be determined not to let him down.

*

The forecast was accurate. Jamie drove with Ben and Karen to his favourite viewpoint for observing the rut. He parked in the turning area at the end of the track and they walked up to the bealach. They continued along a faint downward path on the other side of the watershed and into another glen. Air and earth were saturated; overnight rain had not yet relented and the clouds were down. At a levelling in the path they studied their first objective: the notorious rope-and-plank bridge.

Jamie uncoiled the rope, tied Ben and Karen into it, and set up a belay 'round one of the bridge stanchions. They edged along the slippery planks, white knuckles clenched 'round cold, wet steel cables. It would not have been so bad without the menacing, muddy waters of the Ganges beneath, fed by burns which had swollen to three times their normal girth. Sparkling foam plummeted downward, as bright as white, wild stallions ... raging wild stallions carried on turbulent currents; dark, peaty, ochreous.

The hooded threesome plodded on. Strong boots and gaiters were inadequate; they were taking in water. Thoughts were turning to where they would have lunch, when

"Bloody hell!" Jamie gasped. They pulled up suddenly, on the brink of a cascade of wild water. All three looked down into the blank, staring eyes of a drowned deer hind. Only her head and neck were visible, her body pinioned between water-ravaged rocks. They just stood ...

"Come on, let's keep moving," Karen said.

In a while, Jamie took them over to a *howff* (a natural, stone shelter) he knew, where they huddled and waited for the rain to abate. They warmed themselves with hot drinks but sandwiches would have to wait, following their grisly discovery. After the band of rain had moved through, Jamie raised an arm and pointed: "Down there, that large, lush, flat area downstream from the watersmeet, that's one of the deers' rutting greens. It's used each year as a scene of battle between the stags. Above the watersmeet, where the mountain slopes come steeply 'round to the craggy headwall, that's where I'm hopeful of getting some good recordings. We shouldn't need to go any further; with luck and some patience, we should get the sounds reverberating between the converging slopes and the headwall."

All around, there were sounds of rushing water and roaring stags. Everything was in spate; shafts of sunlit dancing, white ribbons as they sped down the glen. Drips were seeping through gaps in the howff. They crept outside and each got out their insulated mats to sit on, and they sat together on a rock slab. After much fiddling, Jamie seemed fairly happy that the recording equipment was set up okay. He switched it on.

Through binoculars, they watched a group of about twenty hinds, and they all appeared to be settled, but that was to change. A lone stag seemed in control of his harem; however, the ever-alert dominant hind seemed to see it first — a rival stag was above, on the skyline. The hinds became unsettled. The rival stood in the low point of the bealach, framed by swirling mist. He slowly made his way down by the side of the burn, toward the group. Then followed exchanges of roaring, increasing in intensity, as the two ten-pointers drew closer.

Without further ado, the controlling stag made his move; eyeball to eyeball, the two stags strutted parallel to one another along opposing banks of the raging burn. The defending stag looked the more impressive, with his heavy coat matted with peat and peat-drenched heather draped and dripping from his antler tines. He looked fearsome. The two beasts looked away and then exchanged glares. Karen, Ben, and Jamie were enthralled.

The defending stag, which was on their side of the burn, must have been distracted by the hinds and moved toward them in order to settle his harem. This was his opponent's chance; it swam across the swollen burn and made ground toward the group of hinds. The resident stag then took a slow, curving arc to the side and charged at full tilt. Pursuer and pursued. The only escape was by a seven-foot leap, but the contender failed and plunged into the peaty torrent and was swept down twenty feet before being pitched against a protruding bank and clambering out on the far side, where it scampered off. The victorious stag, which just managed to pull up short and thereby avoid a soaking, sent out a triumphant, groaning roar.

"I hope the recording equipment has been running properly," Jamie whispered. Karen and Ben gathered 'round the machine as he replayed the last minute of the recording. Because it was fairly calm, the sonorous booming rang clearly through the cool, October air.

"We should be able to edit out some of the background sounds of rushing water, but it might actually add to the atmosphere," Jamie said.

In their prearranged hourly call, Ben was pleased to report to Callum that they had made some successful recordings.

Tired but happy, the intrepid trio tucked into sandwiches with the last of their coffee before heading back. They were in the last hour of daylight and treated the high-wire act over the Ganges with great respect! From the top of the bealach they could see Callum's jeep parked in the turning area; he had come to greet them. He gave Karen a hearty hug and was obviously pleased to see them back safely.

It had been a special day, an adventure; good tales to tell.

CHAPTER SEVEN

In keeping with their philosophy, the Camerons were generous in rewarding hard work and a job well done. October's deer rut had gone well and this followed a summer of good weather with visitor numbers above average. It was the third week in December and traditionally time for the annual Drumrowan staff Christmas shindig, a time for the laird and his wife to reward their loyal and hardworking team. The Camerons' residence was by then tastefully adorned with Christmas garlands, gold silk ribbons entwined round the wooden banisters of their double staircase, and with draped sashes in the clan tartan. Inside the heavy, oak entrance doors, a crystal chandelier sent shimmers of dancing light over the foyer tiles. All this provided a magnificent backdrop for the forthcoming celebrations.

It was a splendid occasion and every staff member who could make it was there. Two things heralded the start of the evening's festivities. One was the switching on of the floodlights; castellated walls and curved, turreted towers — like the rooks on a giant chessboard — were bathed in shafts of whiteness beamed from the ground. The other prelude of things to come was the strident sound of Highland pipes blown by a tall, kilted piper; it was the good laird himself, Douglas Cameron.

A gong was sounded and the gathering made its way to the Long-room. Catering staff from the café, supervised by Lady Cameron (who prepared much of the food herself), had assembled a lavish buffet and carvery, the centrepiece of which was a spit-roasted wild boar. Foil-wrapped potatoes had been cooked in the big, log fire. The fragrance of pine resin was carried in wood-smoke into drifting candle-smoke and over herbal aromas. Drink flowed as freely as the Bhruie Burn in spate and no one went away until the small hours or was disappointed; it had been a reet good "do."

*

Some weeks into the New Year, on February 21, it was Mo's birthday. A few days before that, she had been in the woods on the higher ground above the holiday lodges. She was crunching her way through the snow when, alert as usual, she caught sight of a mart on the frosted, mossy top of a tree stump. It looked across to her. She stopped; each was as surprised as the other. In that heart-stopping capsule of time, she tried to remember the shape of its gorget. But then, all too quickly, it shot up a pine trunk, moved out along its branchlets, transferred to another Scots pine, and vanished.

Back home in her "pad," Mo looked through photos of the orphaned marts.

"I wonder," she mused to herself, "I reckon I might 'ave seen one of the youngsters we reared! At least it's a good bit o' crack te tell the others when I see them on my birthday."

Mo just invited her close friends 'round to her place for a drink, on the evening of her birthday. Basically these were her workmates, as her brother and sister, who lived in England, couldn't come. Neither Ben nor Karen had been to Mo's home before. He wouldn't have been comfortable going round alone — with vivid, albeit fond memories of their frolic in the heather — but was confident to go along with his partner, Karen.

Mo lived in what was originally a stables block which had been converted into a two-bedroom cottage situated behind the Visitor Reception building. Karen and Ben rapped on her horseshoe doorknocker. Mo swung the door open and greeted her guests with a cheery smile and a bear-hug.

"Good te see ye both."

Ben thrust a bottle of red wine and a birthday card into her hand and she thanked him with a quick, secretive grope of his backside.

"You've made your place really nice and cosy, Mo," Karen said.

"Thanks," Mo replied. "I've been here four years now an' it suits me fine."

They had just got sorted with drinks when Jamie and Davie arrived. While they were being greeted and hugged, Karen and Ben scanned 'round the room. Black timbered beams contrasted with white-painted walls, thick walls with deep window sills. A pair of walking socks gave off a dank smell as they dried by the wood-burning stove, to the side of which stood a basket of birch logs.

"By the way," Jamie announced, "Callum is checking the security alarms on the animal enclosures and he'll be coming along as soon as he's finished. It shouldn't take him very long."

"Thanks, Jamie," Mo replied. "We might as well have some nibbles and some of my birthday cake, providing we leave some for Callum."

Mo led her four guests into the kitchen, where they helped themselves and returned to the "snug" with their snacks. During their second or third drink, Mo played one of her favourite Stones tracks, "Satisfaction," and the evening was turning out to be a good wee gathering of friends.

Into his third can of beer, Ben was obliged to ask Mo where the toilet was.

"It's through the narrow passage at the back of the kitchen, Ben."

"Cheers, Mo."

He negotiated his way down the single step into the passageway, swung 'round, and pitched his face into some scanty, red knickers and bra, which were hanging from a pulley drying-rack!

"By the heck! Mmm," he muttered as he slowly peeled away the slightly warm, damp undergarments. His mind was wandering; he remembered that he was in a building that was once a stable block and wondered where Mo kept the whip and chains. A nervous shiver ran down his spine and he hurried back to the front of the cottage as soon as he could.

With everyone back together, Mo described her recent sighting of a mart. Photos of the hand-reared cubs were passed round. The cubs would be fully grown by that time and Mo did see an adult-sized mart. She couldn't be sure, but Mo thought it likely that she had seen one of the orphaned youngsters and the others readily agreed.

Karen broke the relaxed atmosphere in the snug by asking, "I wonder what the hold up is with Callum. It's half past nine now, and that makes him two hours late."

"Aye, somethin's nae reet," Mo added. "Callum's usually pretty reliable. We should go an' see if he's all reet."

"Good idea," contributed Davie. "I don't mind staying back to take any phone calls," he added, looking a bit worse for wear.

"Fine, Davie," agreed Mo.

Without delay, the foursome donned their jackets, grabbed a couple of hurricane lamps, opened the door, and stepped into wind-driven snow. They hurried over and boarded Mo's jeep. Everything was so different from two hours ago; fine weather had given way to a winter's storm. They knew that no one in their group was functioning well; they had been drinking. Five minutes ago in the comfort of Mo's cottage, they were expecting to go out on a false alarm, have a laugh, and enjoy teasing their gaffer Callum for being so late.

They were shocked by the horrendous conditions; if Callum was out there, they needed to get to him quickly. They drove off in the direction of the holiday lodges. As they watched, the curving string of white guide-lights along the path connecting the lodges went out. Within seconds, all lights in the Reception and adjacent buildings failed.

CHAPTER EIGHT

Turbulent winds whined and thunder rumbled menacingly 'round the surrounding mountains, cloaked in blackness. There was an atmosphere of foreboding all around; the storm was encircling Drumrowan. They drove over the bridge and left the racing waters of the Bhruie Burn. Muted groans from the huskies — animals well accustomed to wild weather — carried across in the force eight. Mo's jeep struck a flooded crater in the track; a screen of soft snow engulfed the nearside of her vehicle and the windscreen, temporarily blinding her. The jeep veered down a dip in the track as Mo fought desperately to regain control, but then there was an almighty crunch and everything stopped.

No one spoke for a minute, before the four occupants gradually stirred and prodded one another. The only casualty seemed to be Jamie, who was in the front with Mo. He touched his forehead and felt a damp, warm stickiness in his fingers.

"Are ye okay, Jamie?" Karen asked.

"Aye, nae so bad thanks, Karen," he replied. "Must 'ave gashed my head a bit."

She leaned forward and gave him her scarf. "Here, tie this 'round to stop the blood."

Fortunately, the engine was still running, the windscreen was intact, and the headlights were still functioning. They revealed the trunk of a Scots pine which had been uprooted and blown across the track.

"Damn and blast it!" Mo sighed. She tried to make radio contact with Callum but could get no reply. She paused to gather her thoughts. "Reet, it's probably best if we split into two teams of two," she suggested. "If two of you could walk back and brief Lord and Lady Cameron of what's happened, the emergency services can be called out from there. In the meantime, there's a chainsaw in the back, so if one of you can give me a hand, I'll try te cut enough of the fallen tree te clear the track. It's likely Callum will be up at the wolf enclosure, so if we can drive up te the next turning area, we'll walk from there."

"Aye, good idea, Mo, I'll give ye a hand with clearing the tree out of the way," Jamie volunteered. With that, he promptly opened the jeep door, apparently fainted, and pitched into the snow. His mates pulled him to his feet and knocked clouds of powder-snow off him.

"Think I'd better walk back down with you and get you indoors, Jamie," Karen offered. She linked arms with him and took one of the hurricane lamps. Mo nodded in agreement as they set off down the snow-covered track in their quest to see the Camerons.

"Take it canny, now," Mo added encouragingly.

Mo and Ben watched the glow from Karen's lamp become smaller and dimmer in the spindrift. They then retrieved the chainsaw and Mo started trimming branches from the trunk, with Ben holding the remaining hurricane lamp. After cutting through one section of the trunk, she straightened her back and took a breather.

"I say, Mo," said Ben, "there's something strange, have a listen."

Only creaking branches and a dull whining of the gale could be heard, as flurries of white flakes were driven across the headlight beam.

"Aye, yer reet, Ben," she replied. "I can't put me finger on it, but there's summat missin'."

In another ten minutes, Mo managed to cut through the trunk a second time, and with a concerted effort, they rolled the severed section of timber clear of the track. They were knackered, but at least they could now be on the move again. The jeep slithered up the track and slewed to a halt in the turning area, a few feet from Callum's parked Land Rover.

"Thank goodness!" exclaimed Mo.

They left their vehicle and followed the blurred traces of Callum's boot prints, which were nearly obliterated by wind-driven snow. Mo stopped. "I've just realised what it is that's strange," she said. "The wolves are silent."

More negative thoughts played on their minds as they continued to track Callum's prints in the wet, white powder. Before long, they could just make out the snow-plastered rocky outcrop near to a corner of the high security fence round the wolves' enclosure. A couple of hundred yards along the fence brought them to the access gate of the compound. Their worst fears were realised; a mature Scots pine had been blown over, crushing the security fence and demolishing the access gate.

Ben swung the hurricane lamp to cast a moving glow over the scene of devastation. From the last of the boot prints lay Callum's spread-eagled body lying sideways in the soft, wet crystals. His left arm was trapped under a bough of the fallen tree. To the side of his head, snow was stained the colour of cranberry.

Instinctively, Ben called, "Callum, Callum, can you hear us?"

Nothing. Mo moved in close and noticed a nasty gash in his scalp whilst feeling for his carotid.

"I can feel his pulse, but it's quite weak," she said.

"What the hell do we do now, Mo?"

"Okay ... we'll need te get back te the walkie-talkie in the vehicle an' try te make contact with Jamie and Karen at the Camerons' residence. We'll take instructions from Lord and Lady Cameron, but we obviously need an ambulance te get as near te us as possible. Meanwhile, Callum always keeps a couple of blankets an' a bit of tarpaulin an' stuff in the back of his Land Rover. I'll take what I need back up te Callum an' do me best fer him."

They headed off for the vehicles to enact the plan.

"We've only one lamp between us, Mo," Ben said.

"Ah, if I could take it, then I could take the chainsaw an' try te cut Callum free. If you could stay with the vehicles an' wait fer help, here are the keys, in case ye need te move the jeep," Mo said.

At the vehicles, radio contact was made with Karen, who explained that Jamie was still rather groggy but was being looked after by Lady Cameron. A three-way conversation then ensued between Lord Cameron, Karen, and Mo. An ambulance was needed and Lord Cameron would phone for one. Mo was informed that storms had affected power supplies to most of the region, and although some telephone lines were still working, not much else was. Mo explained that she reckoned she could cut Callum free with the chainsaw but would report back if the Fire Service was needed. Ben was to stay with the jeep and Land Rover and relay messages. Before finishing, Mo added, "Those are the immediate problems, but there's nae trace of any of the wolves ... over and out."

After the call, Mo gave Ben a comforting hug. If there was anyone who could give the most assistance to Callum, he thought, it was Mo. In his eyes, she was some hell of a woman; he was awestruck by her indomitable spirit. He watched his idol as she gathered the lamp, blankets, tarpaulin, and chainsaw and strode off bravely into the tempest.

*

An hour or so had passed and Ben had become very cold huddled in the jeep. He had slipped into a torpid state — eyes closed and arms wrapped round his chest — in an effort to pretend that all around him was not really happening. He uncurled himself, stirred by loud crackling from the radio.

"Ben, this is Douglas Cameron. Are you okay? Give me a progress report, please."

"Hello, sir," Ben replied. "I can only just hear, you are breaking up. Mo hasn't returned — she is up at the wolf enclosure attending to Callum."

"Don't worry, Ben, I have requested assistance from the local Fire Service and have asked for an ambulance. It will take about forty minutes before they arrive. I've instructed them to go straight up to where your vehicles are parked and proceed by foot to the wolf enclosure. Do you think you could go up to Mo and Callum, or is it too wild?"

Ben's thoughts were that it *was* too wild, but by then his adrenalin level was soaring. "It should be ok, sir. I'll make my way there now, cheers."

"Good luck, Ben. Over and out."

Ben tried to get his stiff limbs moving. Opening the jeep door, his foot snagged in a coiled hemp rope on the floor and his crumpled body pitched into the wet, white crystals. Instinctively, he tossed the hemp coils over his shoulder and staggered off into the tempest.

He didn't know what he was doing; his brain wasn't working, his feet weren't working. Hypothermia was setting in. All sense of time was lost. With every few paces, the wind would buffet him prostrate into the snow. It would have been so easy just to stay there and sleep on that niveous blanket. Only thoughts of helping Callum and Mo forced him back to his feet. Ben was convinced that he had transcended to some ethereal, spiritual plane. After what seemed like an aeon of time, he saw a distant glow; a defiant, hope-filled radiance within the periphery of darkness and doom. The nearer he came to it, the more magical were its powers. It was in fact Mo's lantern swinging above her and Callum.

"Hey, Ben, what a state yer in," called Mo.

He stood rather helplessly as she knocked clouds of powder-snow off him.

She continued, "I've managed te cut Callum's arm free. He's been driftin' in an' out of consciousness, but I've kept talkin' te him."

Ben looked around. Mo had rigged the tarpaulin into a shelter, to the side of which the hurricane lamp swung from an overhead bough, casting distorted, ghoulish shadows. His mind was still numb with cold, but he did manage to explain that help was on the way.

"It doesn't look as if Callum has a spinal injury," remarked Mo, "so I reckon we need te move him down as he's cold and blue. That's good that you've brought the rope. Could ye give me a hand te make an improvised stretcher from the tarpaulin, Ben?"

"Of course," he replied.

She set to work with her bush-knife to cut the hemp into lengths. After a while, Callum was padded with a couple of blankets and bound in a cocoon of tarpaulin; he looked more comfortable than they felt. Each with a rope tether, they made surprisingly easy progress in lowering their friend and casualty along the snow. They looked with relief as lights from the emergency vehicles approached their parked jeep and Land Rover.

"You were amazing up there, Mo," Ben said.

"Ach, not really." Mo shrugged. "But doin' nothin' is nae an option, it can be fatal. You must have a plan, even if it's nae a very good one and if that doesn't work, always have a 'plan B.'"

*

Matron rang the brass bell to signal the start of visiting time at Auchanbhruie Cottage Hospital. Lady Cameron had brought Karen with her to visit Callum. The Ward Sister briefed them on his condition; he had suffered a fracture to his left upper arm, had some severe bruising, and ten stitches held together a big gash in his cranium. He had had a good, settled night and they were told he would have no lasting damage. His speech was fairly coherent and the effects of concussion should go in a day or two.

The ward doors swung open and in they strode. Callum was sitting up in his bed, back-rest set high, left arm splinted in plaster and with a large bandage 'round his head. Lady Cameron and Karen greeted him with a kiss and a gentle, right-sided hug and placed a bunch of grapes on his bedside table. He was anxious to know which animal enclosures had been damaged in the storm. His visitors explained that, although most of the enclosures were intact, the worst damage was on the higher ground, particularly the wolf enclosure, and that many trees had been blown down.

"The wolves, what about the wolves?" enquired Callum, looking pleadingly into the eyes of his visitors.

Their ashen faces conveyed that they were the harbingers of bad news.

"I'm afraid there's no trace of them, Callum," Lady Cameron said as she stretched out a hand to his good arm. She continued, "Douglas has, of course, spoken with the local constabulary and it appears Scottish Natural Heritage will need to be informed, but I'm sure it will all get sorted out."

Karen added comfortingly, "For the time being, everyone at Drumrowan just wants you to mend up as quickly as possible, Callum. They all send their love."

"That's really kind of you all, please convey my thanks back," he replied, a warm smile spreading across his chestnut-brown face.

He was getting tired, so Lady Cameron and Karen said their goodbyes and each left him with a peck on his cheek and went their way.

*

An aroma of coffee drifting from the warming-stand in the Laird's study prompted Douglas Cameron to bring the Deer Management Group meeting to a close. "Do help yourselves to coffee, gentlemen."

He and his colleagues, representing the three neighbouring Estates and the Forestry Commission, pondered over their plan to recapture the wolves. The most likely areas would be searched in as few days as possible, with the assistance of volunteers from the local Wildlife Trust. If the wolves were seen, an attempt would be made to stalk to within firing range and shoot them with tranquilising darts by qualified personnel. A start would be made the following week. Well, that was the plan.

However, for well over ten years, there had been reliable and regular reports of "very big cats" — pumas — roaming free in Scotland and England. These pumas were still roaming wild, so what chance had they with the wolves? No one dared admit it, but there was a better chance of catching a flying haggis.

*

Lady Cameron had arranged a wee "welcome home" gathering for Callum in the Laird's residence. Knowing that McNeish was not one to seek attention, she made it a low-key affair. There was, of course, a full buffet laid out and a big, roaring log fire. It was a good chance to have a good cheery get-together over a few malts — at least that was the intention. In hindsight, it was perhaps not the best time to have such a party. Everyone close to Callum — and many were present at the shindig — knew that his most pressing worry was the whereabouts of the ten wolves which had escaped in the tempest. Indeed, it was on everyone's minds.

A molten-lava glow from the log fire shone along the stone walls of the Laird's Long-room. Adorning the culinary table were several clusters of silver candle-stands supporting columns of waxen radiance, which gave a dramatic under-lighting to white beards, chestnut, weathered faces and which seemed to enhance the curvature of white blouse over breast. Lady Cameron looked glamorous in a long, silken dress with her flowing, fair hair resting over a sash in red Cameron tartan. The kilted Douglas Cameron stood proud in his clan tartan regalia.

Callum was with his friends as he held a dram of malt in his strong fingers. A lot of thought had been put into making Callum's welcome home just right. But it wasn't. There was an undercurrent, not of bad feeling — on the contrary, there was a feeling of genuine love — but it was undermined by a big worry which affected all of Drumrowan and beyond; ten wolves were out there somewhere.

CHAPTER NINE

Three weeks had elapsed since Callum's discharge from Auchanbhruie Cottage Hospital and Karen was driving him back there to have his plaster and stitches removed. Much had happened in that time; Callum had agreed with Lord and Lady Cameron to Jamie's promotion to Acting Head Keeper to cover for his sick leave. This came as a relief to McNeish who, even before his accident, was beginning to feel the effects of many years in a tough, outdoor job. Perhaps his body was telling him that he was not thirty years younger.

In any case, he was only about a year short of his retirement and Jamie was pretty well trained up to take over from him on a permanent basis.

Karen drove carefully back with him from the hospital along the stony track approaching Drumrowan. The front nearside wheel struck a pothole and McNeish winced, clutching his unprotected injured arm. He was grateful for the big packet of paracetamol that the Ward Sister had sent him home with.

Meanwhile, eight miles down the glen and away from the epicentre of drama at the Wildlife Park, Amy and Chris were busy with the increased bed and breakfast bookings at Inverkeld in the run up to Easter. That morning, after serving breakfast to their guests, Chris took his daily stroll into the village to buy a paper.

After seeing the last guests happily on their way, Amy switched the kettle on for a brew before making a start on stripping the bed sheets. Before long, her peace was interrupted when Chris boisterously returned in one of his states of panic.

"Hey, Amy ... just listen to this," he blurted out. "It's the talk of the village ... on the newspaper hoarding ..."

The headline read:

KILLER WOLVES ESCAPE

"It's not covered by the nationals but I was told there's an article in the *Highland Chronicle.* It hasn't been delivered to the newsagents yet, so I'll pick up a copy later on."

He sat down, still out of breath, and joined Amy for a mug of tea. At least every fortnight, they tried to meet up with Ben and Karen for a family meal. Consequently, they had been apprised of the situation regarding the wolves but had obviously been told in strict confidence.

Amy slid a slice of toast to him, saying, "Karen and Ben are coming through for an evening meal tomorrow. It'll be a good chance to find out what is really going on. Do you think wolves are dangerous?"

"I used to think so," replied Chris, "but I've been influenced a lot by young Karen. She studied animal behaviour at university and knows about these things. Evidently, in the European countries, there have been very few wolf attacks on humans and nearly all of those had been by rabid animals, and Britain is free of rabies."

Amy added, "Ben shares her views, in that they both believe in living and letting live. Karen has said that generally, if you do not threaten or attack a wild animal or come between a mother and its young, you are perfectly safe. Anyway, I've the bedrooms to sort out. Perhaps if you would get a *Highland Chronicle* later on, we could go through it over our evening meal."

Chris fiddled on with a thing or two until lunchtime and then bought a local paper. None of their guests had booked a meal that evening, so Amy and Chris had more time to relax after their own tea. Chris finished washing and wiping the dishes and brought two coffees over to join his wife on the settee. She picked up the *Chronicle* and read the front page headline: KILLER WOLVES ESCAPE. She scanned the main points of the article and said, "I might have guessed, with such a sensational heading as that, it's written by Seth Hankin. He's always on the lookout for any juicy gossip. He's unscrupulous; what he doesn't know he just makes up. How he gets away with it is beyond me."

Chris agreed. "Yer dead right, love. He's got a bad name in the village. The locals call him Sleazy Seth, not to be trusted an inch."

They both read the article more thoroughly; it was short on facts and full of fabricated rumour. The couple dozed off on the settee. Eventually they stirred and went to bed in the hope of not being woken by wolf howls at the windowpane.

*

Sunday evening was usually the best time for them to meet up with Karen and Ben, as the weekend guests had booked out and it was generally a quiet evening. At six-thirty, Ben and Karen drove down to see them. They met up and decided to walk through the village and have a bar meal at the Claymore. They went over to a corner table near the open fire and started to peruse the menu. Chris went to the bar to order drinks and caught Joss's eye, one of the Claymore's regulars who was born in Inverdruie, and went over to him.

"Evenin', Joss, what's the crack?"

"Well, Rosie at the bar tells me a bloke has booked himsel' to stay 'ere a few nights at the inn. He just arrived today ... 'ave seen 'im briefly, 'e's a stranger an' one o' those Sassenach types."

"Ye mean like me!" Chris said with a smile.

"Nae," chuckled old Joss, "'e's different. If ye wear a suit an' tie round these parts, ye stand oot like a sore thumb. We reckon 'e's a reporter from one of the nationals. He'll be up te nae good, he'll be tryin' te get a story aboot them yon wolves. Let the animals be, that's what I say."

"Thanks very much, Joss, I hope it all gets sorted out. Take care now, I must be getting back."

Old Joss smiled as he carried on enjoying his scotch pie and ale.

Chris returned to the table with drinks and brought the others up-to-date with the crack. Highlanders Pie was the favourite choice from the menu, and the main topic of conversation was the wolves — at least it made a welcome change to the cost of living.

*

News of the wolves' escape had brought a slight edge of excitement to the Claymore Inn; on several nights a week one could usually hear an animated discussion about them in either the Public or Lounge bar. The wolf situation was beginning to polarise the community into two camps: one with the "shoot to kill" approach and the other with a tolerant attitude of living *with* nature and not fighting it. Shortly after the "Great Escape," it was even feared that some hotheads would be scouring the countryside in armed posses to hunt down the beleaguered animals.

Sleazy Seth's sensational scoop KILLER WOLVES ESCAPE was to be his last literary masterpiece; he was suspended and later dismissed by the *Highland Chronicle* because of "serious professional misconduct."

The newspaper reporter from the City returned back south without a story. He had a torrid few days staying at the Claymore; all the locals regarded him with suspicion, his manner was abrasive, he got their backs up, and they regarded him as an intruder. Consequently, virtually everyone refused to speak to him and those who did said no more than "Nae comment," delivered with contempt. He booked himself out of the inn a day early and returned south.

With their usual good sense of timing, the Camerons, with friends in high places, sent out a press release to the editors-in-chief of the main broadsheets and others, giving a balanced account of the wolf situation.

*

In the weeks that followed, the lupine dust began to settle a little. Ben and Karen had invited Mikel for an evening at the Claymore. Having settled themselves in a corner of the Lounge Bar, Ben and Karen listened as Mikel described a holiday he had in the Carpathian Mountains, in an area inhabited by wolves, bears, and lynx. He explained that, to limit the numbers of cattle, sheep, and goats killed by these predators, local farmers used breeds of livestock guarding dogs such as *cuvacs* and Caucasian Shepherd dogs to deter wolves and bears, which would otherwise be shot to extinction. As puppies, they were reared with flocks of sheep and their traits were of being pretty fearless and very protective — ideal for deterring most bears and wolves; they had proved to have significantly reduced livestock losses in the Carpathian region. Karen and Ben were so taken by his account that they persuaded the shy Swede to relay it to Jamie the following morning.

Having heard from Jamie of Mikel's holiday, Lady Cameron decided to pay him an afternoon call for a chat. She struck the cowbell in the veranda and kicked off her wellies as Mikel welcomed her to his pine lodge. His late father's heavy, wooden Nordic skis and poles were displayed on a wall in the lounge, which was decorated with antlers of red and roe deer and reindeer.

Over cups of herbal tea, Lady Cameron expressed her interest in the use of livestock shepherd dogs, and Mikel willingly explained about them. They were on the same wavelength; both could see the potential for using such methods in Scotland, should the need arise.

"Lady Cameron, with the wolf pack still roaming free, where do we go from here? As wolves are pack animals with a well-developed group hierarchy, that should make the logistics of locating them a tad easier?"

"Please just call me Pippa. If the pack can be recaptured, that's fine, but you and I know that simply won't happen; once the snow cover goes it will be virtually impossible to track them. If that is the case, they will eventually be shot to extinction, just as they were more than two hundred years ago."

"Unless there are non-violent but effective means of managing them," replied Mikel.

"Exactly," she agreed. "Perhaps the use of livestock shepherd dogs may play a part in a many-sided approach to resolving the issue. I will run the idea past Douglas and I'll let you know. Thanks for a pleasant couple of hours, Mikel. You have a lovely home, and I like your reindeer-hide tablecloth!"

"My pleasure, Pippa, you are welcome anytime. Cheerio for now."

In the morning, the Camerons had a long "working breakfast." Pippa brought another rack of toast from the kitchen. The local constabulary had, of course, been informed at the time of the wolves' escape. Although the police were satisfied that no sabotage or other criminal act had taken place, their advice was for the Estate to inform Scottish Natural Heritage. In Callum's absence, Mo and Jamie had pulled together the facts, and under the guidance of Lord Cameron, a detailed report had been sent to the authorities.

"Is there any more coffee, Pippa?"

"Of course, darling," she replied, shunting the coffeepot and toast rack towards him.

"The prospects of recapturing our wolves appear to be pretty bleak," she suggested.

"I agree, love. We had to abandon the systematic searches; it was simply not possible to sustain them beyond those first few weeks."

Pippa added, "It will probably be many months before the effects of predation on livestock can be assessed, yet we cannot afford to just mark time — our farmers need the reassurance that positive things are happening."

She explained about the livestock guarding dogs, and after deliberating over yet more coffee and toast, they took the bold decision to acquire documentation to import and quarantine four such dogs.

*

Over a year had elapsed since the Great Escape, and in that time four cuvac shepherd dogs had completed their quarantine period. Mikel had returned from a trip to Romania, paid for by Lord and Lady Cameron, where he stayed for three weeks on a remote hill-farm in wolf and bear country. There he learnt about rearing and training cuvac shepherd dogs and how they were used.

Douglas and Pippa Cameron had beforehand asked Mikel to take on responsibility for the four dogs (and, of course, be paid for doing so), liaise with local farmers, and deploy the dogs on farms where there was a problem with livestock.

The Camerons were having another of their working breakfasts.

"Well, Pippa, you will know that, as their Laird, I have been visiting the local farmers recently, with Mikel. They say that they have not suffered any more livestock losses than in other years, meaning that whilst predation by foxes continues to be a problem, this has not been aggravated by the wolf pack. Being astute hill-farmers, the locals have been quick to realise that the guard dogs would not only protect their stock from wolves, they would also reduce their ongoing problem with foxes!"

"Splendid," replied Pippa. "I expect Mikel is getting on well with the farmers, as he told me that he once owned a reindeer herd back in Sweden."

"That's right, darling, they respect the fact that he too was a farmer, and they're getting on fine with him." He added, "Like the rest of us, our farmers have noticed a significant increase in the number of tourists about the place, attracted by the mystique of having a wild wolf pack in the region. I am sure that more people are coming to realise that, as with ospreys, red kites, and the like, wild creatures are infinitely more valuable to local communities alive than they are dead. Indeed, three of our farmers are seriously considering upgrading their spare rooms, with a view to doing bed and breakfast from next season!"

He continued with his bowl of porridge after exchanging a loving smile with his beautiful wife. They could read each other so well. He knew from the glint in her eyes that she would use her considerable abilities to assist the farmers with their bed and breakfast plans.

CHAPTER TEN

Jamie decided to have a trip in the mountains on his first day off after Easter. He had arranged to go with Mikel, and their objective was to climb Bheinn Bhan (Ben Vahn, White Mountain), a Munro just beyond the Drumrowan Estate. Jamie had climbed it before but not in winter conditions. The high corries of Bheinn Bhan held a mantle of snow well into the summer every year. Although Jamie had some winter experience, he would never attempt such a peak in winter on his own.

He was in the best of company. Lean, tall, and long-featured Mikel was just as competent and relaxed sledging with his husky team, climbing with his ice-axe, or gliding on Nordic skis as he was walking; he was a real "man of the snows."

It was nine o'clock and Jamie was ready. Ice-axe and crampons strapped to his rucksack, he strode off on his way to call for Mikel at his lodge. A crispness was in the air, a magical stillness with only the animals stirring. He almost had to brush past the magnificent, shaggy Highland cattle that were waiting for warmth from the first rays of sun.

"*God morgon* (goo morron),"whispered Mikel.

Jamie returned the greeting in his friend's native Swedish. They headed off and made good progress up the glen. A couple of steep sections followed, up a narrow, heather-clad path that brought them to the tree-line.

Tzee-tzee-tzee ... tzee-tzee-tzee. "Crested tits!" whispered Mikel. They watched as five or six fed busily from Scots pine cones.

"Magic!" enthused Jamie.

He and Mikel continued for several hundred yards to a large boulder where they laid down their sacks.

"Time for a snack," Mikel suggested. They ate some chocolate and surveyed the terrain; the heather-clad track continued for another two hundred yards before disappearing into the first of several big snowfields.

"Our route should cross that first snowfield and break out onto the narrow ridge on the right," Mikel said.

They finished their snack, donned another fleece under their windproofs, and headed for the snow, hats on and ice-axes in gloved hands. Damp mist swirled over the wet snow as they made the traverse.

"I remember the ridge as a pleasant scramble in summer," Jamie said.

"But not so easy today maybe!" Mikel smiled.

The way ahead was along a snow-plastered, rocky spine which disappeared and reappeared through a grey veil. Its vertebrae were coated with winter's sugary icing. Their aerial highway undulated at first, curving left and right, before tapering into an alpine-like arête. Ice-frosted granite gendarmes stood as sentinels along the snowy crest. A final steepening brought the intrepid couple to a halt.

"I think this is a good place for lunch, Jamie. It's fairly sheltered here, but once we get onto the summit plateau we will be straight into the northerly wind."

"An excellent idea, Mikel."

They busied themselves getting out sandwiches and thermos flasks as a pair of ravens ghosted past in the mist.

Mikel said, "It's also a good place to put crampons on. You will have noticed the snow texture is much firmer up here and that the rocks have become frosted; it will certainly be very icy on the plateau."

"Mikel," enquired his friend, "I assume that after crossing the summit plateau, we will go down the south-west ridge and eventually rejoin our outward path?"

"That is right, my friend, but that ridge should be easier; it is broader and will have lots of good snow and fewer rocks."

Crampons fitted, they continued up the steep uppermost rocks of the arête. Just before emerging into the wind, they glanced left and right; big cornices were hanging over the headwalls of the corries.

They crunched along to the summit cairn, shook hands, smiled, took a couple of photos, and enjoyed their moment. On they continued toward the top of the south-west ridge.

"Aaah!" cried Jamie. He had dropped waist deep into a concealed hole in the snow.

"Jamie, are you okay?" Mikel's half-hidden companion tried to extricate himself, groaning as he did so, but it was no good, the pain was too much. Mikel took his rucksack off and put his arms under his mate's armpits.

"I am going to pull you gently, Jamie, try to help if you can."

He pulled his friend free and they lay sprawled on the ice. More groans.

"Can you stand, Jamie?"

He tried once but fell back in agony. Mikel checked him over; Jamie's right knee was extremely painful and he couldn't flex it.

"You have wrenched your knee and there is probably some ligament damage."

"Feels that way," Jamie said with a sigh. "It's really throbbing."

Staying positive, Mikel added, "We must get shelter from the wind." He swung his axe into the frozen snow and started to make a windbreak 'round his friend.

Before long, the athletic Swede had constructed a low wall of snow round his injured colleague. He then tried to phone the police and Mountain Rescue services, but to no avail; they were in a signal blind-spot. It was obvious that Jamie was immobile and Mikel knew the best option was for him to hurry down to the glen and call out the Mountain Rescue Team. Jamie agreed it was the only thing to do. Before setting off, Mikel wrapped his two-man emergency shelter 'round the young Scot, left him his food and thermos flask, and made sure the youngster drank some coffee.

"I will fly like the wind and we will have you down in the valley before long," Mikel said as he tapped his pal's shoulder, smiled, and sped off.

How Mikel wished he had his skis with him. Snow was starting to fall. Two thirds of the way along the ridge, he stopped to examine the slope down into the corrie. The concave snow-slope was very steep but free of protruding rocks and would take him more than six hundred feet down to the approach path they had ascended earlier. It would save him a great deal of time. He stashed his crampons away, and with flexed knees and ice-axe at the ready, launched himself into a hair-raising glissade. Timeless minutes later, a sharp turn into the slope brought him to a spectacular halt amidst clouds of snow. He dusted himself down, ate a handful of raisins, and continued on his mission.

Meanwhile, Jamie was left to his own thoughts. Snow was falling quite heavily, but at least he felt warm enough. He kept his spirits up by thinking of the camaraderie that was developing between him and Mikel. If there was one person he would trust his life to, he was the man — and he was beginning to realise he was doing exactly that!

He ate his last sandwich and dozed off. Two hours later the coldness woke him. He realised the likelihood of the Rescue Team getting to him before nightfall was slim. The situation started to intimidate him. Snow continued to fall. It would be better, he thought, if he could crawl and slide down the easy ridge and out of the wind. As he stuffed the emergency shelter into his sack, the pain returned, but staying on his backside, he started shuffling his way toward the ridge ...

*

Rescue Team members made their way up the easy south-west ridge in fading light. They carried out a search of the summit area; the improvised windbreak was beginning to get banked up with spindrift and there were no signs of habitation. New snow and wind had obliterated all axe and crampon marks; the plateau was a featureless windswept white expanse. The team conducted a second line-search and made its way over to the top of the difficult arête Mikel and Jamie had ascended earlier. They called down to their colleagues who were climbing the final iced rocks. Falling snow drifted across the lights from their head-torches. After reuniting, the team warmed themselves with drink and food before contacting Base; it was decided to adjourn the search until the morning.

A prompt start was made the following day, which was overcast with more snow forecast. The search area was extended, but after a difficult, tiring day, Jamie could not be found. There was a subdued atmosphere at Drumrowan later that day. With his injury, Jamie could not possibly have moved far, and even if he was basically okay, there was the grim prospect of him having to endure another bone-chilling night on the mountain.

The next day, three rescue teams continued searching in falling snow and poor visibility, with several rescue groups checking the corries on either side of the arête. One group stopped to scan the lower slopes of the corrie; they couldn't believe it — there was a wolf lying between some snow-plastered rocks! Its grey-white coat melded into the snowscape, and its dark eyes met theirs. After a few timeless moments the wolf slunk away. What they then saw was even more amazing.

"Hey, bloody hell, there's our man!"

They hurried forward in the powder-snow; it was Jamie. Immediately, the team doctor dropped to his knees and felt for Jamie's carotid. "He has a pulse, a bit weak, but it's there — great!"

In addition to his wrenched knee, Jamie had a head injury and was unconscious. First aid was given and preparations were made to get him back down to safety.

"It's likely he's fallen several hundred feet down this gully above us, after crashing through the cornice," one of the rescuers commented, and his mates nodded.

The team doctor added, "His head and leg injuries are obvious, but there are no signs of him being bitten or mauled by the wolf. Furthermore, his chest and abdomen actually feel really warm, no doubt as a result of the animal laying across him for an extended period. Amazing, really incredible!" His colleagues expressed their agreement; they were dumbfounded.

CHAPTER ELEVEN

After a couple of days in Auchanbhruie Cottage Hospital, Jamie was back home in his flat near the Drumrowan Reception buildings. His doctor had signed him off on three weeks' sick leave to nurse damaged knee ligaments, which would take months to fully recover. In light of this — and in response to an increase in workload — the Camerons had recruited someone to assist the Rangers. The newcomer was a young Scots lass called Aileen, who was able to start straight away. Lord and Lady Cameron could employ her without delay; her details were already held on file as she had been interviewed before, short-listed, and was nearly appointed in place of Davie, keeper of the small animals.

By the second week of his incapacity, time was beginning to drag for Jamie. There was a rap on his door knocker and grabbing his crutches, he went to answer it. In the opened doorway stood a petite lady clad in working clothes, green wellies, and a green fleece top worn by the Rangers. Curly, mousy locks framed her smiling, brown, lightly-freckled cheeks and green eyes.

Fond memories condensed into a timeless minute. Jamie, dumbstruck, dropped a crutch, banged into the door frame, and started to slide groundward. Quick-acting Aileen pinned her slight frame against him; he was heavier but she was remarkably strong. His second crutch started to slide away.

"Quick, I'll help ye over te the settee," she said.

With Jamie groaning in pain, they lowered themselves onto the settee and continued their embrace, this time with long kisses.

"Aileen, we've not seen each other in years, what a surprise!"

"I've just been taken on as an Assistant Ranger and had heard you were working here. But we'll have te meet up later, I'll need te get back te work."

"Where are you staying?"

"I'm staying in Mrs McGuillvary's flat above the post office," she replied, giving him a card with her phone number on. She retrieved his crutches and gave him another kiss.

"That's great, Aileen, it's really good to see you again. Bye for now."

*

"Cheers!"

Seven full beer glasses clanked together over a corner table in the Claymore. Jamie had been invited along to the local Mountain Rescue Team's social evening, in acknowledgement of his donation to them of a fifty pound cheque. Fiona, a team member of twenty years, started things off by saying, "It's good that our efforts are appreciated, Jamie, especially by someone who is well-equipped and experienced as you are — unlike the halfwits who flip about on the high ground in sandals. It's very generous of you, thanks."

Jamie's eyes flinched with emotion as he felt the poignancy of what he was about to say: "You canna put a price on saving someone's life; it is everything, your very being."

A teardrop rested on the lip of an eyelid, ready to spill down his clean-shaven face. For the first time since his epic adventure, he was reliving what he had gone through. He would forever be acutely aware of his mortality; he had been plucked from the fine, intangible line between the zenith of life and black finality — in the quickness of falling through a cornice. It was all getting too much for the young Scot, but he drew comfort from knowing he was with men and women of the mountains who had seen many serious injuries, shattered lives, deaths; he sensed their empathy with him.

Hamish, the team doctor, deftly moved the conversation on. "We would like to make special mention of your encounter with the wolf in our Accident Report. How do you feel about that, Jamie? Also, when were you first aware you had four-legged company out there?"

There was an air of expectancy as Jamie paused to drink some of his beer. "I do recollect drifting in and out of consciousness and that, early on, a wolf approached me when I was lying in the snow. It came right up to me and lay across my body — she was heavy, the alpha female of the pack, the one we know as *Sheebah.* I can't remember any more."

"That's an excellent account of what happened, Jamie, especially considering the state you were in," Hamish replied.

"What interests me as a medical man," he continued, "is that this wolf's behaviour played a crucial role in your survival; although your feet and toes were very cold, your core temperature was fine. The wolf saved your life, of that there can be no doubt."

"I'm sure Sheebah was protecting me as she would with her own offspring, and also because of the special bond that has developed between us," Jamie said. "She clearly knew exactly who she was protecting; she knows my smell. The whole thing has had a profound effect on me, something I will always treasure."

CHAPTER TWELVE

Mo had arrived early. She and Mikel were sat on the veranda step to his pine lodge at eight-thirty on a balmy June evening, drinking lemon tea. They were waiting for Ben and Karen plus Jamie and Aileen; together, they were to have a stroll in the twilight, to celebrate the summer solstice. Before long, all six were exchanging greetings. Each had brought either water or fruit-juice, a snack, and midge repellent! Mikel and Mo also carried hip flasks.

The happy sextet headed off into the gloaming, two-abreast along a track by the Bhruie Burn as a wagtail acrobatically darted in pursuit of insects. At a fork in the track, Aileen and Jamie had arranged beforehand to strike off left up a sketchy path through some birches, leaving the others to continue along the main track.

"Before we part company," enquired Mo, "are we all goin' te Callum's retirement 'do' next Friday? With the whip-round I organised, I've booked the back room at the Claymore, so I hope you can all make it."

"Sure, Mo, we'll all be there," replied Karen. "It should be really good!"

"We'll leave you two love-birds in peace then, fare ye well!" said Mo, with a sly grin.

*

"We should be clear of the midges by now," Jamie gasped.
"Thank goodness, let's get our breath back and have a drink."

They were above the trees, on a fairly level grassy area with patches of bilberry. A warm, humid breeze drifted into their faces as they stopped and waited for their heavy breathing to settle. Jamie pulled a blanket from his rucksack, laid it on a clear patch of grass and, taking one of Aileen's hands, gently tugged her down to sit with him. He offered her some bottled water and deliberately splashed some across her front.

"Jamie!"

He just looked at her with his cheeky, boyish grin, something she first found attractive in him years ago. She looked at him attentively as a moonbeam reflected in his cerulean eyes. After rehydrating themselves, they laid on their backs and gazed upward to the infinite, cosmic heavens; a full moon was low in the sky; high, wispy cirrus clouds floated over a darkening blue backcloth, laced with a galaxy of stars.

She could feel her clingy white top sticking to every part of her clammy skin. A hand glided down her warm, very moist skin, funnelling and snuggling deep between the steeply rising contours of her braless breasts.

Heavens, she thought, *is this really happening*? *I'm sure he's noticed I'm sweaty and damp. My heart is pounding, he can feel it. My nipples are erect, he is over them. My breasts are rising, filling, and falling... rising and filling ... push your shoulders back, be proud of what you have and let him enjoy.*

With her eyes closed, Aileen had become anaesthetised into nirvana.

*

"Hey, Aileen," whispered Jamie, "wake up." He gave her a gentle prod and tried again. "Hey, wake up, but stay quiet."

Pulling on her partner, she sat up by him and rubbed her eyes.

"Just look over there, Aileen!"

A lone wolf, two or three hundred yards ahead, was trotting along the grassy path *toward* them. The young couple instinctively embraced each other firmly round the waist, not as a reaction of fear but to enhance their shared sense of euphoria.

"It's obviously picked our scent ages ago," commented Aileen. "The breeze is carrying towards it."

"Dead right, my little angel," he agreed, giving her a firm squeeze. As the wolf drew closer it became evident it wasn't alone; they were watching a female with her three cubs, which were struggling to keep up. She continued to approach with a fluent, confident gait. Eventually, just as they thought they would end their days with massive, joint heart-attacks, the creature pulled up.

She sniffed the breeze after giving a snort to clear her nostrils of stale, humid air — but there was not the slightest hint of aggression in what she did and the couple knew it. She made some muted contact calls to her feisty cubs and continued forward alone.

"My smell is familiar to her, but she's coming over to check you out. Just keep your eyes fairly low and look submissive; you'll be absolutely fine. It's my dear friend Sheebah."

"Keep tight hold of me!" *If there was ever a time,* she thought, *of having to place complete trust in your loved one, this is it!*

In typically relaxed manner, Jamie held out his free arm. "Hello Sheebah, it's good te see you again. You saved my life, you wondrous creature, and I think you know it."

He could see the full moon's pastel-yellow reflection in Sheebah's glistening, lemon-centred eyes, as her wet, jet-black muzzle brushed against his arm and body. He gave her a firm one-handed hug, his fingers running through her luxuriant coat. Before diminutive Aileen knew it, Sheebah's tremendous power and weight gently knocked her sideways, as the wolf nuzzled right into her moist neck and licked her salty skin.

Sheebah then returned to her cubs, flopped to the ground, and faced the young couple *just ten feet away,* jaw resting on her folded forepaws. A magical, lupine moon-shadow cast along the ground towards them, silhouetting her long body, noble head, yellow-centred eyes, and alert, triangular ears.

Aileen enthused, "Life can't get any better than this!"

There was no need for Jamie to express agreement; it was obvious. However, he was inspired to say, "Here we are, two key predators — human beings and wolves — each at the top of its food chain, sharing the same ground, having mutual respect, neither feeling any threat from the other, living alongside each other without any conflict. It is tragic that so many people choose to *fight* nature, rather than live *with* it in harmony."

"You can be quite a deep person at times, my man; it's time we started making our way back home."

With great reluctance the couple rose to their feet and rolled up the blanket. Sheebah made some sweet, muted sounds, clearly intended for the two of them. They gazed, awestruck, into her lunar-lit, glistering eyes once more, as if they were embracing a loved one before they departed at a railway station. Linking arms, Jamie and Aileen started back. In fifty yards they couldn't resist one last glance; as they turned, Sheebah and her cubs were making their way uphill, on the other side of the glen.

"Farewell, wild one. Take care of yourself and the youngsters, we'll look out for you again ..."

CHAPTER THIRTEEN

Rosie came through from the bar and greeted the motley gathering as she removed white cloths that were covering the buffet. Callum's friends were enjoying their first drink, seated on the cushioned, dark-stained pew which ran full-length along one wall. Above them hung an old, faded, browned map of the region. Three corner seats were kept free.

A taxi door slammed shut and a minute later, Callum stood in the entrance to the snug, followed by Pippa and Douglas Cameron. They stooped under the low, oak lintel and took their places.

"Hello there, Callum ... welcome!" his friends croaked in staggered unison.

"It's good te be with ye," he replied, his beaming face framed by a shining white beard. He was now free of work responsibilities and his chestnut skin, although creased and weatherworn, had lost much of its tension. Pippa, wearing red Cameron tartan slacks with matching waistcoat over a white blouse, slid a malt in his direction.

"What have you rascals been up to then?" he enquired. "What's the crack?"

There was a floodgate holding back a flood of dramatic news to be told, and Callum's question had breached the dam. The summer solstice sextet looked at one another excitedly. Aileen couldn't contain herself any longer and launched into a detailed account of their amazing encounter on the moor.

Mo added, "Isn't it exciting that three cubs have been seen — they must be the first Scottish wolf cubs born in the wild in a *very* long time. It's terrific news!"

Jamie continued by saying, "It was the alpha female of the pack, Sheebah, my guardian lifesaver when I had my accident."

Aileen concluded her tale by adding that she and Jamie last saw the wolf and her cubs heading uphill on the other side of the glen.

"Hey, that would be about the direction we were in, at the time!" exclaimed Mikel. Even the placid Swede was becoming animated. "Furthermore," he continued, "Mo, Karen, Ben, and I heard spine-chilling howls being exchanged somewhere along the skyline — *Canis lupus!"*

He stood and his forefinger roved over the old map behind him. "It was there."

Callum got to his feet and peered at where Mikel's finger rested. "Ah!" he elucidated, "perhaps it was meant to be — the mountain from where you heard those wondrous howls is called *Sgurr a' Mhadaidh* (Scoor a' Varti). It means 'hill of the wolf!'"

Douglas Cameron chinked his glass and rose to his feet. "Before we make a start on the sumptuous spread, would you kindly be upstanding, folks. Here is a toast to wish our dear friend Callum a long, happy, and healthy retirement.

"Cheers, Callum!"

A hearty "To Callum!" filled the cosy, candlelit snug. The shy old fox thanked his friends and, in typically unselfish fashion, deftly diverted attention away from him by proposing a second toast: "To *Canis lupus,* their freedom found!"

"To *Canis lupus,* their freedom found!"

THE END

Sheebah

www.ingramcontent.com/pod-product-compliance
Ingram Content Group UK Ltd.
Pitfield, Milton Keynes, MK11 3LW, UK
UKHW041920190726
13854UKWH00003B/1349

9 781452 034003